1812

1812

Jeremy and the General

A Novel by JOHN IBBITSON

Maxwell Macmillan Canada

Maxwell Macmillan Canada
1200 Eglinton Avenue East, Suite 200
Don Mills, Ontario
M3C 3N1

Canadian Cataloguing in Publication Data
Ibbitson, John
        1812 : Jeremy and the General

ISBN 0-02-954025-9

1. Canada - History - War of 1812 - Juvenile
fiction.* I. Title.

PS8567.B25E5 1991   jC813'.54   C91-095068-7
PZ7.I23Ei 1991

Cover Design: Brant Cowie
Cover Illustration: Wes Lowe

Printed and bound in Canada
∞ Printed on Acid Free Paper
6 7 8 9 0 TCP 5 4 3 2 1 0 9 8

This book was written for Grandma Boyd,
and in memory of Grandma Ibbitson.

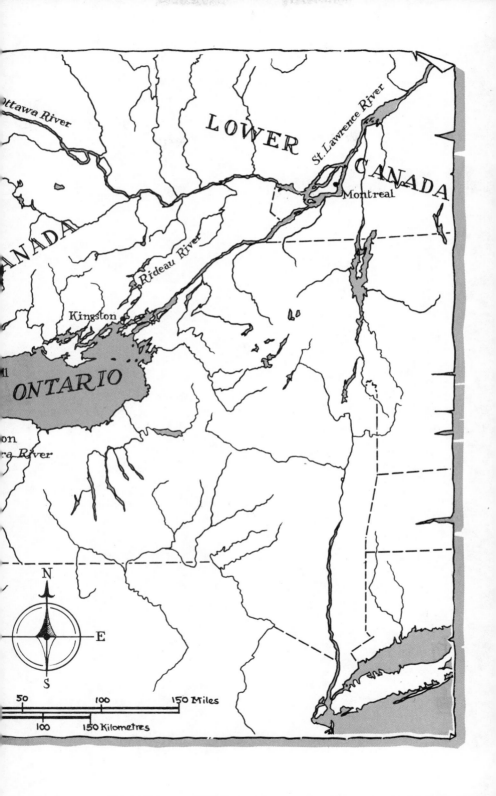

1

They were expecting me to cry. I had seen tears in Uncle Will's eyes and Aunt Amy had been crying since Tuesday.

I should have cried too. She was my mother. But I couldn't.

"Thou knowest, Lord, the secrets of our hearts. . . ."

Mr. Morrison was no minister—his farm was up the road. But he knew the service and there wasn't a minister for miles, so he said the words.

"We therefore commit her body to the ground—earth to earth, ashes to ashes, dust to dust . . . ." Dirt dribbled from his hand and rattled across the rough pine wood.

The women stepped away, took each other's arms, and began the walk back to Uncle Will's house. The rest of us reached for the spades that leaned against the elm. Uncle Will took my arm.

"You don't have to, son."

"I want to."

No one spoke after that. We sank our shovels into the soft spring earth beside the grave and heaved the earth into the grave below. There were six of us, and it didn't take long. I never noticed when the last of the coffin disappeared.

When it was finished I stood over the two graves for a moment—the fresh, new one of my mother, the old grey earth beside it where my father was buried—and pretended to say a prayer. The wind tugged at my coat, and a fine drizzle began to darken the earth. I turned away and joined the men walking across the field to the house.

Most of the farmers along Yonge Street still lived in the log cabins they'd built the year they cleared the land. Our log cabin hadn't changed much in the fifteen years since I was born in it. But Uncle Will and Aunt Amy lived in a proper house, with two bedrooms and a stove inside and even lanterns at night. It was crowded now in the main room, but not too crowded to hold the dozen neighbours who stood uncomfortably and sipped on tea and tried not to show how long it had been since they'd tasted sugar cookies. People talked among themselves—about the late spring, the crops, the war we might have with the States, but not about death.

"You'll stay with us tonight, Jeremy." Aunt Amy dabbed a handkerchief across her eyes.

"I think I'll stay at the farm."

"Oh no." She lowered her handkerchief. "You can't stay there all alone. Will . . ." She pulled at his sleeve. "Jeremy wants to go back to the farm. To his—to his parents' farm. He mustn't do that."

"Wouldn't you rather stay with us for a bit, son?" Uncle Will offered. "You know you're welcome."

"Someone has to feed the animals. And I want to be alone tonight." And I did.

"Well, he's fifteen, he can take care of himself." Uncle Will smiled. "I'm sure he'll manage."

"I don't know, I don't know." Aunt Amy's handkerchief fluttered about her face. "It doesn't seem right." But she began drifting toward the tray of cookies, which meant she'd given up.

"I don't blame you, son," said Uncle Will, as I pulled on my coat. "I'd want to get away from all this, too. We've put cheese and some meat in the root cellar. Be sure you eat."

"Thanks." I wanted to leave, but he stepped forward and took my arm. Uncle Will was a big man—tall and broad and heavy. He always stood close to other men when he talked to them, as though he wanted to remind them of his strength. I didn't like it.

"We have to go to Richmond Hill tomorrow," he said quietly. "There are . . . some legal matters. Your mother gave Mr. Robinson the papers."

I nodded. Legal matters. I hadn't thought about that. What were we going to do—about the farm, about me?

It was a muddy walk home. I wasn't used to wearing shoes. Boots were what you needed for open fields in May. But I ignored the mud. There were things to consider.

What were we going to do about the farm? I couldn't run it alone. And I didn't want to run it. I hated the farm.

I stopped in the field. *I hated the farm.* It echoed inside me. I'd never known that before. Oh, I'd said it every day. *I hate this farm,* I'd say to myself, as I struggled with the hay for the cows, or spread the manure across the fields, or fought with a chicken for her egg. *I hate this farm.* It was like part of breathing.

But I'd never really known it until now. Known it absolutely. I hated the farm. I hated farming. I'd always hated it. So had my father.

My family came to Upper Canada in 1784, after the American colonies rebelled against England. My father and my Uncle Will were the sons of a farmer in New York. The two brothers stayed loyal to the King when rebellion came, and because they were loyal the Yankees threatened to put them in jail as traitors. So they left, both still in their teens, and came to Upper Canada. The Americans who came north after the war were called Loyalists, and they got grants of land.

I don't know much about their first farm, but it must have been poor, because when the government began opening the land north of York for settlement, they sold the farm and took land on Yonge Street, about twenty miles north of the town.

They each had two hundred acres, side by side. But you'd have thought their farms were on opposite ends of the earth. My Uncle Will was born to farm. His crops ripened faster, his cows were fatter, his children were fatter too.

My father worked from dawn to dark and it never seemed to do any good. I heard someone whisper once that the only luck he ever had was getting mama as his wife.

He met her in York. She was the daughter of a miller, and people thought she was too good for him (I heard Aunt Amy say that once), but she married him anyway.

I don't know if she knew what she was getting into. We lived in a one-room cabin. The stone fireplace gave us light and heat for food—and smoke to choke us until our eyes watered. She kept the house clean, and looked after the cow and the chickens and the pig while my father fought with the land and lost.

One day he was working in the field when suddenly he grabbed his chest and fell down and didn't get up. That was seven years ago. I don't have much of a memory of him. All I remember is a man sitting at the table at night, his face shadowy in the firelight, staring silently at his hands.

Mama should have given up the farm and gone back to York, but she stayed. This was where God had put her, she said. She worked from before the sun was up till after it set. She worked in the field and in the house and in the barn until the lines on her face seemed to deepen as you watched her. She didn't talk much when she worked, and she never sang, but I sometimes heard her humming to herself, some song I didn't know.

I worked too. At first there wasn't much I was good for, except bringing in the eggs and sweeping the floor. But I was always big for my age—I had my Uncle Will's shoulders, mama used to say—and by the time I was ten I was doing a man's work.

Uncle Will would lend a hand when he could, or send his son Seth. We'd help each other with the harvest, mama working in the fields beside the men while Aunt Amy shook her head and muttered that it wasn't right.

There was no school I could go to, so mama taught me to read and write and do sums. We had only the Bible to read, but we read it every night. I guess there wasn't much laughter on the farm—mama didn't think much of people who cackled like hens, as she said. But it was comfortable at night, the two of us together, me reading the Bible out loud, or writing out sentences with chalk on an old slate, mama correcting my mistakes.

I'd noticed her getting thinner, and she held her side sometimes and set her face against showing the pain, but she never said anything about it, and I never asked. Then last Thursday, we'd just finished getting the field ready for the spring planting when she leaned on her hoe and said she felt dizzy. I helped her to the house, then ran to get Aunt Amy. Mama lasted less than a week, getting weaker and weaker. She was hurting inside, but there was nothing we could do. By the end we were just hoping she'd stop being in pain.

So they were both gone now, buried on their own land, at the foot of a hill beneath an elm tree. And I was alone.

I stood in the yard between the house and the barn. The low grey clouds had created an early twilight. The tree beside the house creaked in the wind that curled around me and made me shiver. The drizzle had turned to rain, a thin, cutting rain that stung my cheeks. I turned away from the wind and rain and walked to the house.

Inside it was dark, and that was fine. I stoked the fire and pulled a chair up beside it, then wrapped a blanket around me and sat in the chair, waiting for the warmth from the fire to reach inside me. The grey light from the window outlined the shadow of the table. I looked at the table and thought of my mother and cried.

The light from the morning sun woke me. I uncurled myself from the chair and stretched stiffly. There were chores to do—the cow had to be milked, the chickens and the pig fed. I was still in my good clothes; the wool trousers scratched against my legs and I was anxious to get out of them. But Uncle Will had said we were going to Richmond Hill for some business, so I left them on.

I was just coming out of the barn with the milk when Uncle Will's cart trundled down the twin ruts of our path, pulled by a dapple-grey mare Uncle Will owned and everybody envied.

"Are you ready, son?" He seemed impatient, restless.

"Right there." I hurried to the root cellar with the milk, slopping half of it over the sides of the pail and some of it onto me. I ran to the house, where my cheese and bread sat waiting on the table. No matter how restless Uncle Will was I needed that cheese and bread—I hadn't eaten properly in days.

It was the first good morning after a week of bitter weather. The air was moist and fresh, the rain from the night before glinting off the grass and fences in the cool May sun. I munched on my bread and breathed in the scented air. It seemed hard to believe there'd been a yesterday, with a funeral and rain and cold tears.

But Uncle Will seemed gloomier today than ever. Worse—at the grave, he had tried to comfort me. Now he just made me feel uncomfortable. He gripped the reins tight in his hands and stared silently at the back of the horse's head.

"Why are we going to Richmond Hill, Uncle Will?" I asked finally, more to break the silence than anything.

"I told you yesterday, there are some legal things to settle." Uncle Will glanced at me quickly, then back at the horse. "Your parents left a will with Mr. Robinson."

The Robinson mill was the only mill for miles. People brought the grain they grew in their fields there, sometimes in carts, sometimes on their backs. They went away with ground flour—the only real reward for a season of work. James Robinson built the mill in the nineties, and grinding people's grain for them had made him the richest man in the township. What's more, he could read and write and do sums, which most people couldn't, so he took care of a lot of personal business, too.

"What's in the will?" I'd never seen a will before.

"I don't know. Nobody knows what's in a will, until it's opened." He shrugged. "Though of course, everything will have been left to you."

I knew that shrug. It was the shrug a farmer gave just before he tried to steal your cow from you. It was the shrug everyone gave when they wanted you to believe they didn't care, but they did. I knew that shrug—something was going on.

"Have you thought about what you're going to do, Jeremy?" Uncle Will asked, gazing ahead down the road.

I gazed down the road too. "Nope. Not really."

"Well, you're fifteen, now. And you're full grown. You're big for your age, and strong, and ready to work."

I nodded. Around here, as soon you were big enough to work you worked. Maybe on your own farm, maybe on someone else's. There wasn't any other choice, unless you left and went to work in a village.

And what would I do in a village? What was I good for? I could get work as an apprentice, maybe, at a blacksmith's or merchant's. None of it sounded better than farming.

" . . . and of course there's the question of the farm." I blinked. I hadn't been listening.

"Sorry?"

"I said—" Uncle Will gripped the reins tighter. "I said, there is the question of the farm. I mean, it's yours now. . . ."

I nodded. It was mine. Only I didn't want it.

"But . . . " Uncle Will rubbed his forehead. "I'm not sure what you're going to do with it."

"Whatcha mean?" I gave him a swift look. He'd been thinking about this.

"Well, you're a strong boy of course, no doubt about it." Uncle Will slapped my knee. "You've got your grandfather's build—you must be near six feet, now—and his eyes."

I grimaced to myself. Why did people always talk about your eyes? My mother said I had her father's eyes. My father'd said I had *his* father's eyes. They were just eyes—

sort of grey and too wide apart, if you ask me.

"Though you remind me of your mother, too." Uncle Will continued. I groaned. Another adult comparing me to other adults.

"You have her hair of course. Fair, like hers, and wild—do you ever get a comb through it?" I ran my hand through my hair, which I did a hundred times a day, though it never did any good. "And you've got her cheekbones and her nose." He chuckled. "Your father always said the thing he loved most about your mother was her nose. I told him—well, never mind." He blushed slightly.

"About the farm . . . ."

"I was saying you're big for your age, and strong, but you can't run a farm, now can you?" Uncle Will raised a sceptical eyebrow. "I mean, you're too young. And you're all alone."

The question was back again. What was I going to do? I waited for Uncle Will to go on, but he didn't have anything more to say.

"What should I do?"

He shrugged again. "I'm not sure. I've been thinking about it, but I'm not sure." He shook the reins. "Let's wait until we see Mr. Robinson."

We didn't speak after that. Uncle Will went back to staring at the road, and I stared at my hands. I'd always known what was going to happen to me—I was going to work on the farm I hated until mama was too old, then I would take it over. Now she was gone, and I didn't know what my future held.

It was only a few miles from the farm to the mill, but

Yonge Street was never easy to get along, especially in the spring. We probably would have got there faster walking, but Uncle Will was over fifty now, and men over fifty liked to sit, even if it meant taking longer to get someplace.

But we reached the mill finally. It was a wooden building, two storeys high and narrow, with a large wheel on one side. We climbed out, and walked inside.

We were in a storeroom full of great bags of oats and flour, and air full of dust that drifted in the sunlight streaming through the window.

"Hello!" Uncle Will shouted, and in a moment Mr. Robinson came out—a thin, grey little man in a black coat.

"Hello, Mr. Fields." He shook Uncle Will's hand. "A pleasure as always."

"This is my nephew, Jeremy," said Uncle Will. "Thelma's boy."

"I'm so very sorry to hear of your loss." Robinson tilted his head to one side. "Your mother's father and my father were the best of friends. She was a brave woman."

"I told Jeremy that his parents entrusted you with their will." Uncle Will seemed restless.

"Yes, it's in the office. Follow me."

Robinson disappeared through a door near the back, and we followed. Just as we were about to go in Uncle Will stopped, and gripped my arm.

"Jeremy..." He swallowed. "I want you to know—I loved your father and your mother. They were part of our family, and my family means more to me than anything in the world."

I nodded to show I understood, but I didn't. It seemed

to me such a strange thing to say.

We went in, and found Robinson sitting at a desk piled with papers, most of them rolled up and tied with red string. He motioned Uncle Will to sit, but my uncle went over to the small window, and looked out. This room was too small for him.

Robinson pulled one of the pieces of paper from the pile, and cleared his throat.

"Your mother left a will, Jeremy, and asked me to take possession of it. I'll open it now, if you wish." I nodded.

He untied the string and opened the letter. Quickly he scanned the lines, then passed it to me.

"It was drawn up in York, and of course it's all in legal language, but briefly, your mother willed her estate—that is, the farm and all her worldly possessions—to you."

He offered me a thin smile. "The will also provides that, in the event of her death before you reach the age of twenty-one, I am to act as trustee for the estate."

Uncle Will stepped toward the desk. "Jeremy and I were talking on the ride in. We agreed that it would be quite impossible for him to manage the farm on his own."

I looked sharply at Uncle Will. I may have thought that, but I'd never said it.

"Quite so, quite so," Robinson agreed. "We have a dilemma, in this regard."

Uncle Will cleared his throat. "Jeremy, I would be willing to purchase the farm from you. With the money, you could get a start of your own in life. You could help me farm, if you liked, or learn a trade, or . . . ." His voice trailed off.

"As your trustee, Jeremy, I must say I think this would be

for the best." Robinson smiled. "Selling the farm would surely be the wisest thing to do."

"I think . . . twenty pounds would be a fair price, don't you?" Uncle Will looked to Robinson.

"Yes," Robinson nodded. "Twenty pounds would be fair indeed."

Twenty pounds! The farm was worth five times that. On bad days Mama would talk about selling—she'd say she was tempted to take the hundred pounds some man had offered her and go back to York.

"Twenty pounds is too low." I glared at Uncle Will. He turned away and looked out the window again. I swivelled around to Robinson. "It's too low."

Robinson rubbed the side of his nose. "Under normal circumstances, I would say yes. But," he smiled apologetically, "the farm is not in prime condition. Your parents were unable to clear much of the land. And it would not be easy to find anyone with the capital to purchase a farm in the middle of spring planting."

"I think it's quite reasonable, Jeremy." Uncle Will moved and reached out a hand, but I shrank back. "It's quite reasonable under the circumstances."

"You must also understand, these are difficult times." Robinson stepped from behind his desk. "You know there is talk of war. The British and French are at each other's throats. And now the Americans are involved. If hostilities should break out, we could be invaded, our villages torched, our farms burned by Yankee troops."

"You'd do all right," I shot back. Anger flushed my face. I could hardly breathe. I could hardly think. I hated the farm. I didn't want it. That's what I'd said to myself. But this . . . this was wrong. They were stealing the farm from me. They were *stealing* my mother's farm.

"I won't do it. I won't sell." I swung from one to the other. "You can't do this to my mother. You're taking her land from her."

"Jeremy . . ." Uncle Will reached out his hand again, but I shrunk back. "Your mother's dead. I wish that weren't so, but it is. This is the best thing now."

"No! I won't let you do it!" My shout echoed against the bare walls of the empty room. The two men stared at me, shocked.

Robinson cast a quick glance at Uncle Will, who nodded. Robinson walked back to his desk and held up the will.

"Jeremy, under the terms of this will, I have full power of attorney as your trustee. That means I can do whatever I feel is best for you, with or without your consent. I'm sorry you don't agree, but I feel your uncle's solution is in your best interest."

Uncle Will took a leather pouch from his coat and walked over to Robinson's desk.

"I took the liberty of bringing money with me. I believe you'll find twenty pounds there." He dropped the pouch quickly on the desk as though the leather were burning his hand.

"Oh excellent! I've drawn up the necessary papers. If you'll just sign. . . ." Robinson held out a sheet of paper to Uncle Will. He paused for a moment, his eyes closed, his face tight. Then he grabbed a quill from Robinson's desk, dipped it in a bottle of ink, and scrawled his name across the bottom. Robinson handed him a worn-looking slip of paper.

"Here is the deed to the farm. I'll have the contract witnessed later. The property is yours."

Robinson picked up the pouch, removed several coins, and slipped them into his vest pocket. Then he turned to me. "And here, Jeremy, is fifteen pounds. My services in this matter entitle me to a small commission, but the rest is your inheritance."

"I don't want your money!" I backed toward the door. The room seemed to be tilting. I was just standing there watching as they took away mama's farm. I was so helpless, so useless. . . .

"Jeremy, let's go home." Uncle Will reached for his coat. "We can talk about this on the way back."

"No, not with you. I hate you!" My hand, groping behind me, found the door knob. I flung the door open.

"You thieves!" I screamed. "You stole our farm! Damn you, you dirty thieves!"

I ran through the storeroom and out into the morning sunshine. The light was blinding. I shielded my eyes, and stumbled along the road toward my home. I cried out curses against Uncle Will, against Robinson, against the world. I swore revenge against them, swore I'd kill them, swore I'd win back my farm.

But I knew the words were empty. There was nothing I could do.

3

For a while I half-ran, half-stumbled down the road back to the farm. Rage washed down me, and back up again.

Traitor! Liar and traitor! Thief! Lying thief!

It was exhausting, and I finally had to stop. There was a tree beside the road and I leaned against it, slid my back down the rough bark, and cradled my head in my hands.

Memories and emotions swirled around inside and collided. My mother . . . the funeral . . . Robinson's grey, thin hand . . . Uncle Will closing his eyes before he signed . . . the farm . . . .

I had to stop. I had to get control. There was no good in this, no good in just hating and running. I had to think, to plan. But it was so hard.

I clenched my fists, tightened the muscles of my face, tried to push down the feelings. But I couldn't. They were too strong. I sobbed, choked, my chest shuddering with each breath.

I don't know how long it went on. When it was over I felt empty, drained. I wanted to sleep.

But I couldn't give in to sleep. I forced myself to

straighten up. It was an hour's walk back to the farm, and standing here wouldn't make it any shorter.

I sweated as I trudged down the road. The spring rains had turned much of it to mud, which sucked at my shoes and made it harder to walk. There was no wind, and no company except the blackflies that swirled around my head. Blackflies in May could drive you mad, but I ignored them. Sometimes, as I passed the farms, I could see a farmer walking along the furrowed rows of his field, casting seed from the pouch hanging at his side. Sometimes his wife would be with him, or she'd be moving about the farmyard, tending to the animals. No one waved. Farmers are too busy in the spring to notice strangers on the road.

My mind was clearing. I'd never felt rage until today, and I was embarrassed. Mama would have been angry at me. She always said that nothing was worse than losing yourself to your feelings.

I cleared my throat loudly. I had an hour free, and I might as well use it. It was time to make a list.

Mama always told me there was no such thing as a bad decision. The only bad thing was not to make one. She said if you looked at things clearly and made a choice, and stuck to that choice, everything would turn out all right in the end. And if it looked as though you'd made the wrong choice, ignore it, because you can never know how things would have turned out, really.

Mama never had time for people who complained. We weren't put here to be happy, she said. We were put here to serve the Lord and not act like fools.

Just know your mind. I could hear her words in my head. *Just know your mind and stick to it.*

That's why, for as long as I could remember, whenever I had a problem I made a list. Once you made a list, I found, you'd know what choice you wanted to make. You'd be ready to choose, and once you chose, like mama said, the rest just happened.

I started my list. What was the first thing to put on it? *You don't want to farm.* That's what I'd been thinking about most since the funeral. That had to go at the top.

What next? *You've lost the farm to your uncle.* I clenched my teeth and pushed down the anger. It was a fact. It had to go on the list.

You want revenge. I thought about that. I did want revenge—I could taste the need for it in the back of my throat. I wanted to hurt my uncle. I think I wanted to kill him.

But what could I do? They hung you for killing people, and I didn't want to hang. I couldn't fight him legally—he and Robinson had all the signed papers; what did I know about the law?

"You can't get revenge." I said it out loud, to the blackflies I guess. It was hard to say, but I had to say it. Things only became true once you said them out loud. There was nothing I could do to my uncle that wouldn't make things worse than they were now. *You can't get revenge.* I added it to the list.

You want to get out of here. I stopped in the road. I hadn't thought about that before, but I knew instantly it was true. I had to leave, leave the farm, leave everything around here, get out.

My mama had a map that her father gave her. She kept it folded up at the back of the family Bible, but sometimes she'd take it out and spread it on the table and show me the world—England, France, Russia, even Japan.

I learned all the countries and their capitals off that map. I used to dream in my bed in the loft of our cabin of going to Europe and seeing London. Or Paris—where Napoleon ruled France and most of Europe.

I thought of the map on the table. All the strange countries. What I would give to see them all! Maybe the army or the navy . . . I shuddered. I'd heard stories about life in the British navy. They treated you like a dog and you died like one. The army probably wasn't much better.

But maybe there were other ways. Maybe I could get on a merchant ship. Or go into the fur trade! Everyone knew tales of the traders who crossed the continent in canoes and lived with the Indians, and lived like the Indians too.

It thrilled me to think of it. No more farming! No more fields and animals and manure. I'd be free.

My walk turned into a trot. I wanted to get home—no, not home, the farm wasn't home any more. But I wanted to get there, get my things.

I'd made my list. I'd made my choice.

It was time to get away from here.

I was somewhere in the North, punching my canoe through a cauldron of whirlpools and rapids, when the sound of horse's hooves pushed into my dreams. I whirled around. Uncle Will's cart was right behind me.

I hopped to the side of the road and swore at myself. I didn't want to see him. I'd been determined to get off the road and hide if he came along. I was too angry, too ashamed at what he'd done to me. But here he was. I had to face him.

"Whoa!" He pulled on the reins and the cart slowed and stopped. The sun was behind him and his dark form loomed over me. I shaded my eyes against the glare.

"Get in." He gestured to the seat beside him.

"No."

"It's a long walk."

"I'll walk it."

"I know you're angry—" he began.

I cut him off. "I'm more than angry." I took a step toward him, raised my fist, then dropped it. What was I doing? What could I hope to do?

"Get out of here." I jerked my fist at the road. "Go on, get out."

He raised himself off the seat.

"Don't you talk to me like that." His voice hardened. "I don't take that from anyone."

"What are you going to do?" I tried to keep my voice from cracking. "What more can you do to me?"

He paused, half out of his seat, one foot out of the cart. Then he sat back down.

"I'd feel the same way," he said tonelessly. "I'd want to kill me, if I were you."

"I do want to kill you." The fury was stirring in my gut again, rising up through my chest.

"You know why I did it?" he asked.

It stopped me. I hadn't expected that.

"Why?"

"Survival." He leaned back against his seat and tilted his head to the sky. I could see his face now, lined and weary and hard.

"We're all just hanging on here, all of us. Even me. I've done well, but I have debts, and I have a family to feed, and I have things I want in my life before I die. I need that farm. I need it more than you do. You're like your father—you don't have a feel for the land. It doesn't mean anything to you, like it does to me. I need that land. And now I've got it. I don't like how I got it, but that will fade."

"It won't for me."

He looked back down at me. "Maybe it won't. But it's over. There's nothing either of us can do."

We stared at each other for a moment, looked into each other's face, read each other's mind. I did understand. It didn't make me hate him less, but I knew him now. He wasn't my uncle any more. He was my enemy. And I was his. We seemed to agree on that together, silently, as though we were forming our own contract.

"What are you going to do?" he asked finally.

"Leave," I replied. "Go south, maybe to York. Maybe travel."

He reached into his coat pocket and pulled out the pouch with the money.

"You'll need this."

I took a step back. "I don't want it."

He smiled. "Very noble, but you'll need it anyway." He threw the pouch to the ground and took up the reins.

"You'll be gone in the morning?" The cart lurched forward.

"Yes."

"Don't bother to feed the animals," he called back. "I'll have Seth look after it."

And he was gone.

The pouch lay in the mud at my feet. Fifteen pounds. Dirty money. They'd raped my inheritance and left me with fifteen pounds. I picked up the pouch, wiped off the mud, and shoved it into my hip pocket.

I tried not to think of it as I continued down the road.

It was hard to sleep, but when I did the wear of the past days caught up to me. The sun was high in the sky when I opened my eyes.

I washed myself quickly in the big metal basin we used for keeping ourselves and everything else clean, shivering as the cold water ran down my back. I only had two woollen shirts and a couple of pairs of rough woollen pants to my name. One pair had a hole in the knee, and I pulled them on, and the oldest shirt. The good clothes went into a satchel, along with my mud-caked shoes (I'd been wearing my father's leather boots around the farm for years), my wool coat, a knife, a tin cup, a hard bar of my mother's soap, the rest of the bread and cheese, and the money.

What else? I looked around the room that I had lived in all my life. There were things I wanted to take—my mother's Bible, which listed the births and marriages and deaths of everyone in her family for four generations, the hand-held mirror she would look into each night before bed, shaking her head at what she saw, the picture of Christ the Shepherd and his flock that was the only thing on our walls that had no purpose—but I left them where they were.

They belonged here, and I didn't. Not any more.

It was well past noon when I stepped out of the house. I stopped once, swung my eyes across the yard between our house and the barn, then turned my back on it.

At the end of our path I paused. Yonge Street twisted and curved its rutted way both north and south. North it led to the Quaker farms and then to Lake Simcoe. Beyond that was only forest. South it led to York, only twenty miles, but slow going. My parents had made the trip in Uncle Will's cart a few times, but they'd left me to tend the farm. Now I'd see it for myself. I shifted my satchel on my back, and started out.

I planned to take my time; there was no hurry. There were villages on the road, and inns I could stop at if I wanted. I'd go as far as I felt like, then stop at an inn, stay there for the night, and go on to York the next morning. After that . . . who could know what came after that?

Walking was pleasant. A cool breeze cut the heat of the sun. Yonge Street was little more than two ruts, and sometimes it was even less, just logs laid together that could knock the teeth out of anyone riding a cart over it. But it made no difference to feet, and I walked along without trouble, craning my neck to make out the robins and blackbirds and crows that filled the air with their calls.

The land was like that around my own farm: low hills with farms on either side of the road, and dark forest beyond. Not all the land was cleared, and sometimes I walked under canopies of branches that arched across the road and blocked the sun. I didn't meet a soul. This was a busy time of year for settlers, and no one left their land unless there was good reason. The road was mine.

When I reached Richmond Hill I ducked my head and ran past the mill and the half-dozen other buildings that were there. It felt good to have Robinson behind me.

After a couple of hours walking I came to a creek, swollen with the spring runoff. The crude wooden bridge— just some logs tied together—had been washed out. I took off my socks and boots and waded across the creek. The tug of the water almost knocked me over, even though it only came up to my knees. On the other side I sat down in the shade of an oak tree and ate my cheese and bread. The water from the stream was cold and fresh. I dunked my head in it, and laughed for no reason when I shook my head and the water sprayed around me. I couldn't remember the last time I'd laughed.

As the afternoon wore on and my legs began to wear out the walking became less fun. I'd passed several inns, but hadn't stopped. Now that looked like a mistake, for the next one seemed a long time coming, and I was ready to quit.

I started to worry. This was strange country—everything from here on in would be strange. Who did I think I was, running off like this? I was only fifteen years old—too young for adventure.

I began to think of the farm. I wished I'd taken the Bible with me. I'd never cared much for it before—it was what I had to study from—but now, for some reason, I wanted to look at it, look at the names inscribed in the front, the names of my father and mother and me, look at the map with all the capitals.

Maybe I should go back to the farm. I could work for my uncle, maybe get the farm back some day. At least I knew the farm, knew the people there. It was home.

These thoughts came back to me more and more as I walked, and each time I shook my head and tried to walk a little faster. There was no going back. I had made my list and my decision. I had to stick to it. I would never work for a man who had cheated me. The future was down this road. An inn would appear soon. Keep walking.

But walking was getting harder. My right foot was rubbing against the rough leather of my boot; the thin wool sock gave little protection. With each step it became more painful. I stopped at a tree stump and took my boot and sock off. A large blister had formed on the side of my foot, just below the big toe. There was nothing I could do. I put the boot and sock back on and kept going. Before long I was limping, trying to rest my weight on the right side of my foot to keep the pressure off the blister.

The fields were grey and the sky darkening when I finally reached the crest of a ridge and looked down into a deep valley, where lights glowed just beyond the bottom. I felt like shouting for joy, but I only whispered a thank you to the sky and began stumbling toward the lights.

It was dark in the valley when I reached the bottom. The lights were closer now—I could make out an inn up ahead, maybe a couple of houses, too.

I was hungry, and the thought of supper made me walk faster and ignore the pain of the blister. It had been a long day, but the day was almost over.

I heard the stream before I saw it. The water rushed over

rocks, fast and dangerous. In July it would be just a creek, wandering south to the big lake. In May it was a torrent.

But I could see a bridge, and as long as there was a bridge, the river could roar all it wanted. When I reached it I rested one foot warily on a log and pushed. The wood creaked and rocked. This wasn't safe. I should go back.

But the lights of the inn glowed on the other side. It would be warm there, and there would be a bed and food. The bridge had survived floods before. Surely it could stand the weight of one more traveller.

I stepped carefully, ready to jump back in a second. But the bridge held. I walked forward slowly, grasping the rail. Water flecked beneath me in the moonlight, inches from my feet.

And then . . . I'm not sure. There was a crack, and suddenly the logs were sliding out from under me. I teetered, tried to get my balance, saw the stars swirling in the dark sky above.

And then there was water, all about me, cold, sucking at my breath. I fought back at it, kicked my legs, clawed myself toward the sky.

And then a sharp pain pierced my head, and a brilliant light flashed across my eyes.

And then I remember nothing.

Three or four different kinds of pain arrived at once. My head pulsed with pain. Pain stabbed at my side. And a wet, chill pain crawled across my skin. I was half awake, half unconscious, completely confused.

The voices seemed to come from far away, maybe from a dream.

"I heard something . . . there . . . it's just an animal . . . no . . . there! . . . something there! . . . Dickson, Spruce, go see. . . . Yes, sir. . . . There's a boy down here! He's hurt . . . Ward, lend a hand. . . ."

Arms reached around me and pulled. The pain in my side stabbed sharply. I cried out.

"Careful with him. He's hurt. . . ."

I was lifted up, handed to one set of arms, then another, until I felt the hard earth under my back. I opened my eyes, tried to lift my head.

"Are you all right, boy?"

I touched my side and winced. A bruise maybe, maybe worse. My head throbbed, but the fog was clearing.

"I'm all right." I looked up. A half-dozen figures clustered around me. One of them held a torch. In the flickering light I caught the dull glow of brass buttons and red cloth.

"You're soldiers?"

"Second company, first battalion, His Majesty's 41st regiment. Now who are you?"

His accent was strange—like a Methodist preacher who'd come by one summer and preached in a field for hours. English accent, mama had said, different from ours.

A tall man stepped forward and looked down at me. "Yes—who are you?"

I could see him clearly in the light of a torch. His coat was red, brilliant red, and his trousers were snow white. A long, silver sword glinted at his side. There were rows of brass buttons, and gold braid on his shoulder, and on his head a tall, tubular black hat with a capped front. He was the most magnificent-looking person I'd ever seen. And his voice. Low, calm, a different, cleaner accent than the others. Everything about him said command.

I tried to rise, but my knees were rubber. Two soldiers hoisted me upright. Once I was standing, my legs seemed to get their bearings.

"I'm Jeremy Fields. Sir." He seemed the sort of man who was used to "Sir."

"You should be dead, young man. We found you wrapped around an old tree, beside the river. Did you fall in?" He was about thirty years old, maybe more, with fair skin and dark hair. Something of a smile played around the edge of his mouth, as though he found this all a bit amusing, as though he found everything a bit amusing.

"I was crossing the bridge." I rubbed my head. "And it

gave way. I tried to swim. . . ." Suddenly I felt, or didn't feel the satchel. It should have been on my back. I reached around, groping behind me. "My satchel! Did you see my satchel?"

"Nothing, sir," a soldier replied. "There was just him."

I groaned. The money was in the satchel. And my clothes. Now I had nothing.

"Bad luck," the officer shrugged. "Never mind. We'll find something dry for you to wear. You can sleep with the men tonight. At any rate . . ." He turned to a soldier who had stripes on his arm. "We can't go any farther with the bridge out. We'll have to return to the inn. Sergeant, form the detachment."

"Yes sir!"

Muskets rattled and clinked as the men arranged themselves in a single line. I hadn't noticed the horse, black as the night, standing silently a few feet away. The officer took the reins and swung himself into the saddle.

"Maitland, look after the boy."

"Aye, sir. Detachment, quick—march!"

The men moved forward as one. The sergeant grabbed my arm and half-dragged me along. It was hard to match their steady pace, but I did my best.

It was only a matter of minutes before we reached the inn. I cursed my luck. I had gotten so close. . . .

The detachment halted before the door of the inn. Maybe half a dozen horses and oxen and carts were tethered in front, and a babble of voices drifted through the door to the outside. Strange, so many people in one place, and not a church.

"Detachment, at ease." The men lowered their muskets. The officer dismounted and turned to the old sergeant.

"You're in charge, Maitland."

"Sir!"

The officer opened the door to the inn. I glimpsed faces and food and mugs, and then the door shut again.

Some men leaned up against a post, some others rested on their haunches. I stared in fascination. All these men, in these beautiful clothes, handling their guns like walking sticks, laughing and swearing quietly at each other, as though they'd seen all the world and this place was the dullest part of it. Maybe they had. Probably it was.

Maitland, older than the rest, with a red face and grey hair, paced slowly about, his head down, occasionally glancing up and peering into the night. When he got close to me I decided to speak.

"What's the officer's name?"

Maitland glanced at me. "He's Captain William Stanton, but you can call him 'Sir.'"

"I call everyone older than me 'Sir.'"

Maitland grinned. "Do you? Well brought up, are you? Well don't call me 'Sir,' because I'm a sergeant, and if you call a sergeant 'Sir' you'll soon have an aching head."

"I already have an aching head."

It was the wrong way to talk to a soldier, I guess, but I was too tired and sore to care. Maitland didn't seem to mind.

The door opened. The officer—Stanton—appeared. "Maitland. Bring the lad in."

"Sir!" He motioned to me and we stepped forward together.

I had never seen anything like this room. There were half a dozen long tables, each with ten chairs, and most of the chairs were full. A large stone fireplace crackled with flames from birch and maple logs. On one side of the room there was a short wooden bar with kegs and mugs behind it, and a woman—thin, grim, with black hair in a bun and no smile. Stanton motioned me to follow him and we wound our way through the tables to the bar.

"Madam, this is the boy I was telling you about."

The woman glared at me. "You say the bridge is out?"

I felt as though I were to blame. "Yes. It gave out from under me."

The woman shook her head. "Well, that's it. There's nothing we can do until the river goes down. I'll have no travellers from the north for a while. Or any going north, either. Damn the luck."

I'd never heard a woman swear before.

"Bad luck for us both. I wanted to go north." Stanton nodded to the men at the tables. "May I speak to these men?"

"We always welcome an officer of His Majesty's infantry." It sounded to me as though she didn't mean it. But she reached up and rang a brass bell hanging over the bar. "Gentlemen! Your attention, please! Captain William Stanton, of His Majesty's 41st regiment, would speak with you." A hush fell over the room.

"Gentlemen." Stanton's eyes swept across the room.

Some men gazed back at him curiously. Others kept their eyes on their food.

"Gentlemen, I am pleased to be able to speak to you. My men and I have tried to reach as many farms as we could over the past two days, but there is too little time and there are too many farms.

"Gentlemen, we may soon be at war."

There was little reaction. A few heads bowed lower. Someone muttered a request to God for help.

There'd been talk of war, of course. Britain was fighting for its life against Napoleon in Europe. They were trying to starve him, blockading his ports. Except the Americans were neutral, and traded with who they liked. So the British were stopping American ships bound for Europe. Sometimes they boarded Yankee merchant ships and took back British sailors who'd run away and were now American sailors. The Americans threatened war unless they stopped.

That was the reason the Americans gave. Most people around here figured the real reason was that the Yankees wanted to grab British territory in North America while the British were too busy in Europe to fight back. And no one really thought the British could stop them.

"For those of you who haven't heard," Stanton continued, "The United States of America has threatened war against Britain over our naval blockade of Europe. Already there are reports of state militias forming to march against Upper Canada. We could be invaded in a matter of weeks. Every man will be needed if we are to repel the invasion."

The men at the tables shifted and looked at each other.

They knew that if there was war they'd be called to fight, and they didn't seem too eager.

"And what," came a voice from near the fire, "makes you think we can 'repel the invasion'?"

Stanton paused for a moment, seemed about to speak, then stopped. He looked at the man near the fire.

"I know what you're thinking. There are ten of them for every one of us. Their president has told his people victory will be 'a mere matter of marching.' You wonder why we should fight, when the fight is clearly lost."

He paused. Only the crackling flames of the fire disturbed the perfect silence. The British officer had asked the only question that really mattered.

"I know that is what you think," Stanton continued, "and my answer to you is this: With all my heart I believe we can defeat the invaders."

"Defeat them? How?" came a voice from the back.

"We have four advantages over the Americans." Stanton counted them on his fingers. "First, we are defending, they are attacking. They must meet us on our own soil, far from their homes. If once their advance is checked, their enthusiasm for this war will quickly fade.

"Second, they are a volunteer army. They have not been properly at war since their secession nearly forty years ago. They will be facing trained, experienced British troops.

"Third, the Indian tribes have joined us. The Shawnee chieftain Tecumseh has formed a confederation of all the Indian tribes of the mid-West. They have promised to fight with us. The Americans are terrified of the Indians.

"And finally—" Stanton lowered his hands and stared straight at the men. "Their generals are either old and tired veterans, or ambitious politicians after glory and votes.

"We, on the other hand, have General Brock."

Brock. I'd heard the name. General Isaac Brock, the man in charge of the British troops in Upper Canada. Nobody knew much about him.

"I have served under Brock in Europe and in the West Indies." Stanton gazed about the room. "He is a great leader, loved by his troops, decisive and brave. If there is any man who can destroy the Yankee armies, he is that man."

"This is no time for us to be making war," said a farmer with a thin black beard huddled over his plate of stew. "We have farms to tend to."

Stanton looked at him impatiently. "Your crops are planted, aren't they? You have families to look after things. What will become of your farm if the Americans conquer us?"

"It'll become an American farm." The farmer shrugged, and returned to his stew.

Stanton looked from table to table.

"If you're afraid that I'm here to call you to arms, then fear not. Your own militia officers will see to that when the time comes. Whether you fight is not my concern. Although," he said quietly, "many of you have parents or grandparents who came to Upper Canada to escape being American. They loved their king and the country of their ancestors. Perhaps that love has died."

He paused for a second, then squared his shoulders. "I am here, gentlemen, to look for volunteers to join His Majesty's army."

"What?" The men looked startled. "We're farmers, not soldiers," someone called out.

"Indeed you are, but what of your sons?" The half smile that seemed always to play around the edges of Stanton's mouth returned. "Perhaps you've been wondering what will happen when you're gone, with too many children to share too little land.

"I am offering you a solution. We need volunteers to fill our ranks, especially now. Any able-bodied man who wishes to join the army will receive clothing, food, wages, and a chance to serve his king—often in climates much more hospitable than this one.

"I will stay at this inn until three o'clock tomorrow afternoon. Speak to your sons. Speak to the sons of your neighbours. Have anyone who wishes to enlist come here.

"Thank you gentlemen. God save the King."

"God save the King." A few called out the words stoutly, a few muttered them, the rest were silent.

I slept with the soldiers in the stable that night. Only officers enjoyed rooms in inns. Someone brought me some food, and someone looked at my side and head and told me I'd live. Maitland rubbed some oil on my blister, which he said would help.

I didn't think I would be able to sleep. I had so much to think about. My money was gone—what was I going to do tomorrow? Where would I eat? Where would I go?

"Maitland?" I whispered, to the dark figure that huddled in the straw beside me.

"Go to sleep, boy," he grumbled back.

"Maitland, would they take me in the army?"

He was silent for a moment. "How old are you?"

"Eighteen."

He chuckled. "I said I was eighteen, too, and they decided to believe me. Yes, lad, I've no doubt they'll take you. Do you want to die?"

"No!" I was startled.

"Soldiers die. Before that they eat bad food and sleep on damp ground and march from dawn to dusk. Then they fight and die. Is that what you want?"

I looked into the darkness. "What else is there for me?"

"Nothing, I suppose," he sighed. "There was nothing else for me. You only become a soldier when there's nothing else. Now sleep."

And I slept.

6

"How old is he?"

"Eighteen, sir."

"Hah."

Stanton looked me over suspiciously, as though I were a piece of livestock not worth the asking price.

"So." He offered me a mock bow. "You've decided to join His Majesty's army. In search of glory and honour, and a shiny red uniform?"

I shook my head. "No sir. I've got no money."

The smile darted across his face and was gone. "Well, an honest answer. Still . . ." He frowned. "I should reject you. You're too young and too impertinent."

"Please, sir." I tried to stand the way the soldiers stood when called to attention. "I work hard. You won't be sorry."

"Won't I?" He sighed. "Well, I suppose we are in no position to turn away volunteers. It would seem you're the only one we've got."

All day we'd waited for men to arrive. None had. I'd overheard the innkeeper grumble that farmers were so afraid of being forced to join the army that even regular customers were staying away.

"Very well," Stanton shrugged. "Maitland, you seem to have adopted this boy. Do keep him out of trouble, won't you?"

"Adopted . . . ?" The sergeant started to protest, but gave up at a glance from Stanton. "Yes sir." He glared at me, but I just grinned back. I liked this sergeant.

"Sergeant, if you would . . . ." Stanton turned his back to the men and walked over to the innkeeper.

"Detachment, sling arms! Move to the right in columns of route!" The soldiers fell crisply into formation. Maitland pointed to the back, and I trotted to the end of the line.

Stanton ended his conversation and strode over to his horse. Maitland stepped forward and saluted.

"Detachment formed . . . *sir!*"

"Thank you sergeant." He nodded to the innkeeper, and raised his right arm.

"Detachment . . . forward . . . *march!*"

We were off to York.

My side ached, and it wasn't long before the blister on my right foot reminded me it was there, though Maitland's oil had helped. The road often gave way to deep ravines, dark and swarming with mosquitos, that we seemed to plunge into and crawl out of. Still, Yonge Street was in better shape here than north of the inn, and I was getting used to walking. There were more farms along this road, and every now and then we were halted and moved to the side to let a cart pass.

Once we passed an old farmer in his field who dropped his hoe and stood stiffly at attention, hand raised in salute, until we had gone by. Stanton saluted gravely in return.

More than once we passed young farmers who turned their backs and tried to ignore us. If Stanton had hoped the sons of the Loyalists would rise to join the army and defend their homes, he must have known now he was wrong. And I knew he would have done worse the farther north he went. Most of the farms near my home weren't even settled by Loyalists. They were Americans who came up here looking for land. If Upper Canada became part of the States, they'd go back to being American, just like they'd been before. Not something worth fighting about.

Late in the afternoon Stanton called a halt and ordered a thirty-minute rest. The soldiers dug into their knapsacks for food, but I had no knapsack. Maitland grudgingly shared the last of his food with me. All anyone had was some hard biscuit and some tough beef you had to chew forever before you could get it down your throat.

"Learn to enjoy it, lad," Maitland grinned. "You'll be eating enough of it, from now on."

"How far to York?" I asked him.

"And hour's march until we see it. An hour more to the garrison. Eat and be quiet."

The sergeant was almost right. Not long after we started marching again the farms ended, and we walked through a broad swath of forest, untouched by an axe. Then suddenly we were on the other side, at the crest of a ridge. In the far distance a spire poked into the hazy air.

York.

To the south the sky merged with the darker blue of a lake, a huge lake with no southern shore. This would be Lake Ontario, one of the great inland seas that stretched from Lower Canada all the way to the middle of the continent. I had seen them on the map, but never thought about what they looked like. I knew this lake was one of the smallest, but I had never imagined there could be so much water.

If it had been up to me, we'd have run. I wanted to explore this capital of Upper Canada that I'd heard so much about and walked so far to reach.

But it wasn't up to me, and no one else seemed in a hurry. The sun was almost behind the trees when we approached the first farmhouses that marked the outer limit of the town.

"Look smart, men," Stanton called out. "They're counting on us to save them. Let's be soldiers."

Much of the land now was just open field, with the odd road crossing Yonge Street east and west, and the odd house where the corner formed. I'd expected more. The houses were grander than our log cabins, with wood clapboarding and shingled roofs, but still they were just houses. I'd never seen a city, but I expected busy streets and grand buildings. One of the men said the main part of town was to the east, and I could see buildings off in the distance. But we wouldn't be going near there—the garrison where the troops lived was well to the west of the town.

When we did pass a house people would come out to look at us. Stanton would nod his head to the women. The rest of us were told to keep our eyes front.

We were almost at the lake when we turned west onto a narrow road. Suddenly Stanton ordered us to halt. Another column of troops was approaching. And what a column! It seemed to go on forever. I counted fifty men. An army!

"Where are they going?" I asked Maitland, as they marched by.

"It doesn't matter where they're going," he shot back. "When they get there, they'll turn around and march back. And stop asking questions. It's impertinent, as the captain says."

Soon we reached the garrison. A wall—they called it a palisade—of wooden poles maybe twelve feet high stretched from the lake to the road, and then west. We passed through wooden gates into a large yard about two hundred yards wide by one hundred yards deep. There were a dozen buildings, mostly large log houses with a door and two windows. Near the edge of the lake was an even larger building, two storeys high, called the blockhouse. A Union Jack fluttered in the breeze beside it.

Most of this I discovered later. My first impression was of noise and movement, of soldiers marching, turning, of sergeants shouting orders, of officers striding purposefully from one building to another. They all looked as though they knew exactly what they were doing, but what they were doing was impossible to tell.

"Detachment... *halt!*" We were standing in front of one of the log buildings.

"Sergeant." Maitland stepped forward and saluted Stanton, who dismounted. "I suppose you will have to find our new recruit a home."

Maitland looked glum. "Yes, sir."

Stanton turned to me. "You will be asked to swear an oath, and once you have sworn it you will be a soldier. You will also be given a shilling, which I am sure you will not spend well. Do you understand?" I nodded. "Say 'Yes sir.'"

"Yes sir."

"Good. You will be a private in the 41st Regiment of Foot. It is a proud regiment, and I expect you not to disgrace it."

"No sir."

"You are the only recruit in this garrison and so Sergeant Maitland will have to train you as best he can. What matters is, you will be a soldier, and will be treated like a soldier and expected to act like a soldier."

"Yes sir."

He locked his eyes on mine. "I do not normally accord such attention to a recruit. But you are the first colonial from Upper Canada to join this regiment. Perhaps you will show us how much—or how little—your people are made of."

I forced myself to meet his gaze, but said nothing. For an instant, his half-smile returned. Then he looked away.

"Sergeant, dismiss the men."

"Sir!"

Stanton stalked across the yard to the blockhouse. The men headed for one of the log houses. Maitland called it a barracks, and when I entered it smelled of sweat and leather. Beds lined each wall, enough to sleep twenty men. But there were already twenty men in this barracks, and I was twenty-one. Maitland pointed to the floor by a stove at one end.

"There's your bed, lad. There'll be a blanket for you, but pallets are in short supply. I hope you're not a restless sleeper." He grinned and left.

I sat myself down on the floor beside the stove and tried to be comfortable, but I knew comfort was a long way from here. Still, at least I was by the stove.

"Hey, you!"

I looked up. He was big, with a red face and muscles straining the cloth of his tunic.

"What makes you think you can sleep by the stove?"

"The sergeant said I could."

"You'll block the heat. Go crawl into the far corner."

I flushed. Who was he, to order me about? "No."

He leaned over me. "You'll go crawl into the corner, and if the sergeant asks you'll say you like it there. Do you understand?"

I looked at the other men. They watched, but said nothing. A couple of them grinned.

I got up and walked to the other end of the barracks. The man laughed. My skin burned with anger, but I said nothing. I was the stranger here, and he was bigger than me. This was no time for fighting.

I crawled into the corner and took off my boots. The blister was bigger than the day before. I stretched out on the floor and closed my eyes. The rough boards stuck into my shoulder blades. *Get used to it*, I thought, *it's your new bed.*

The men began to clean their boots, unpack their knapsacks, joke with each other. Many of them just lay on their beds, staring at the roof. There'd be food, sometime, and nothing to do till then but wait.

"Welcome to the army, lad," someone called out. "It only gets worse from here."

I wondered what he knew.

Mostly I remember feeling tired. The first goal of any soldier is to find a way to rest, and recruits get less rest than regular soldiers.

The hours weren't so bad—I was used to rising at dawn on the farm. It's what you did during those hours. Every minute there was work, hauling logs to build a barracks, cleaning your uniform and polishing your boots, dragging garbage to the lake, painting, cutting, scraping, brushing . . . .

And marching. We marched everywhere and back. We marched wearing packs on our backs that left you aching or numb. The other men were used to it, though they hated every second. I hated every second and I wasn't used to it. I was constantly falling behind, constantly hearing the lash of Maitland's tongue.

"Come on, Fields, get going! You think you're on a stroll? This is the army, you useless sod!"

I had to learn to load a musket in less than a minute—and there are twenty steps to loading a musket. I had to learn to pack a kit, and unpack it, and polish boots until my eyes shone in them, and get used to saluting anyone who looked important.

To be honest, I think I liked it. I enjoyed learning the precision of foot drill—each step exact, precise, each soldier doing the very thing he was supposed to, when he was supposed to do it.

I enjoyed taking orders. It meant I didn't have to make any decisions. So much had happened, so many things I'd had to decide. I was tired of deciding. It was good to just work and sleep and march and let someone else do the deciding.

I had two complaints. One was my bed, or rather the floor with one thin blanket that I slept on. On cold nights I slept on the floor with the blanket over me. On hot nights I slept on the floor with the blanket under me. Either way, I ached in the morning.

The other complaint was MacPherson. He was the one who had forced me to sleep away from the stove, and it seemed to be a sport for him to make life difficult for me. MacPherson was the kind of man who'd stick a foot out to trip you when you passed, then roar with laughter when you fell, as though it were funny. He loved to steal my food or mess up my kit, then tease me about it all night.

I tried to ignore him. I had too much to learn and too much work to get through to let him bother me. And anyway, he was the biggest man in the regiment, as well as the ugliest.

But there were worse things in the world than being teased by a stupid man. And I had my own uniform and my own musket. I had to wait three weeks for the uniform, but it was worth it. I'll never forget that afternoon when I pulled my arms through the tunic and felt the rough wool scratch my back, and felt the brass buttons rub against my fingers.

"Well look at him," someone grinned. "You'd think he was a soldier."

The musket—"Brown Bess" the soldiers called it—took even longer to get, but that was because Maitland didn't trust me with it. Week after week I practised, pouring in the powder, ramming the ball and wadding down the muzzle, aiming, firing, doing it again, but I was always too slow for Maitland, and too poor a shot.

"The safest place to stand in a battle would be wherever your musket was pointing," he'd say in disgust, and make me do it again.

Then one day, near the end of June, we were in a field firing at targets when Maitland came up behind me.

"You'd better keep that one, Fields," he said finally. "It seems to like you."

"You mean it's mine, Sarge?"

"You're a soldier, aren't you?" he growled. "You need a musket. Haven't you heard we're at war?"

"War?" The men lowered their weapons and stared at Maitland.

"That's what I said. The Yankees declared war. Well, it's what we expected, isn't it? Now get back to your practice. And aim well, this time."

From that moment on we lived on gossip and rumour. Where were the Americans? What were they doing? Where were the British reinforcements?

Everyone was a general. Some said we'd retreat right

away to Kingston and give up Upper Canada. Others said no, we'd retreat right back to Quebec City and wait for the war in Europe to end. Others thought we'd fight for York. No one seemed happy about our chances of winning, which is bad news if you're a soldier.

The Americans, we heard, had two great armies preparing to invade. One was forming on the Niagara frontier, the other was on its way to Fort Detroit. It was hard to say which threat was greater. If the Yankees crossed at Detroit and took Fort Malden at Amherstburg, people said everything west of York would have to be abandoned. If they crossed at Niagara, York itself would fall.

Whatever was going to happen, we wanted it to happen soon. June was almost over. The days were hot and getting hotter and there was nothing to do but practise and wait. Waiting made tempers short. There were fights among the men. Sometimes they were planned, behind the barracks when the officers were out of sight. Men would bet on the winner. Sometimes they weren't planned, and two men would hammer at each other in the barracks with their comrades shouting and cheering them on until a sergeant arrived and broke it up.

I kept out of the fights. There was no point to them. And I had no experience in fighting.

So when I did get into the brawl with MacPherson, I was as surprised as anyone.

Things were going from bad to worse with him. In a hundred ways he tried to make life hard—making fun of me, pushing me, stealing things and hiding them. Some of the older men tried to watch out for me—maybe they had sons of their own—but mostly the soldiers kept to themselves.

But I could live with MacPherson, or thought I could. Until the blanket disappeared.

I noticed it as soon as we returned to the barracks after evening drill. I always kept the blanket folded against the wall. But it was gone. The only thing I had to put over me or under me at night was gone.

MacPherson was sitting on his bunk, taking off his boots. I walked over to him.

"Give me back my blanket."

He looked up. "What're you talking about?"

"My blanket's gone. I want it back."

He grinned. "Is your blanket gone? Poor lad."

I felt the anger rise from my stomach. I'd put up with this great, stupid man long enough. "Give it back. Now."

He got up, slowly, still grinning. Standing together, facing each other, he seemed as wide as he was tall. I may have been big for my age, but no one was as big as MacPherson. "I don't have your bleeding blanket," he said slowly, still grinning. "And if I did, I'd never give it back."

"Give him his blanket, MacPherson," someone called out irritably.

"Go on, MacPherson, give it back."

MacPherson spread his arms. "If it's gone, it's gone. There's nothing I can do."

I didn't think, didn't plan anything. I just threw myself at him. It caught him by surprise. He staggered back. I flung my arms around his waist and pushed. Off balance, he couldn't stop himself. We lurched down the length of the barracks, like two crazy dancers, while the other men watched in amazement.

We fell together in a heap by the door. I started hitting at his face, pounding at him. He tried to hit back, but I had his arms pinned to the floor with my knees. I was on top, and winning. It was hard to tell which of us was more surprised.

"Atten . . . *shun!*"

Maitland's bark cut through the air like a whip. The men leaped to their feet. MacPherson and I untangled ourselves and jumped up, puffing heavily. Blood dripped from MacPherson's nose.

Maitland stared at the two of us in disgust. "I don't care what started it. All I want to know is who started it."

I stepped forward. "I did."

He couldn't hide the surprise. "*You?*" He scowled. "I told you men if there was one more fight in this barracks I'd make you pay. I meant it. You're confined to barracks until further notice. Fields, grab your kit and come with me."

I avoided the eyes of the men as I walked back to pick up my knapsack. There'd be plenty of marching for them tomorrow, thanks to me.

But when I turned back, they all seemed to be grinning. Maybe they thought it was worth it to see MacPherson go down.

Maitland paused at the door. "I don't want to hear a whisper from this barracks. If I do, there'll be trouble. And MacPherson—"

MacPherson stiffened. "Yes, sergeant."

Maitland's voice was gentle, almost kind. "MacPherson, how does it feel, to be licked by a fifteen-year-old boy?"

He didn't wait for an answer, but grabbed me by the arm and hauled me out the door.

"Now you've done it," Maitland snapped, as we marched across the parade ground. "I warned you all I'd report the next man caught fighting, and it would have to be you. And the captain told me to keep you out of trouble. We're both in for it now."

"I—"

"Shut up! I don't want to hear it. I've heard them all, and it's always the same."

We reached the blockhouse. Maitland marched inside, leaving me to wait outside and think about what was in store for me. Then he came to the door and motioned me inside.

Captain Stanton was seated at a desk in a small room at the back of the blockhouse. His eyebrows raised when he saw me. "Sergeant Maitland, what have we here?"

"Private Fields is charged with disorderly conduct, sir. I entered Barracks Four to discover a fight in progress. The fight was between Private Fields and Private MacPherson. Private Fields admitted starting it. Sir!"

"*You* started it." Why did everyone seem so surprised that I was in a fight?

"Yes sir," I nodded.

"Against MacPherson?"

"Yes sir."

"You seem to have come out of it remarkably un-scathed."

"The same cannot be said of MacPherson, sir," Maitland offered, deadpan.

Stanton's smile played across his mouth, but he forced it back into hiding.

"This is a serious offence, Fields. Striking a fellow soldier. Quite grave. And you were coming along so well."

He gazed at me for a long moment. "We can hardly send him back to barracks. He's clearly a bad influence on the men. Maitland, you know what I was talking to you about?"

Maitland's eyes widened. *"Him,* sir?"

Stanton nodded. "Possibly. What do you think?"

Maitland's face clouded. "I'm not sure, sir. He's very young."

"Agreed. But he said to choose one of the men, and Private Fields is one of the men." He turned back to me. "Tell me, private, can you sew?"

I shook my head. "No sir."

"Can you cook?"

"Not really, sir."

Stanton frowned. "Can you at least make a pot of tea?"

"I think so, sir."

"Hardly ideal," Stanton sighed. "Still, very little is ideal in this war, and he learns quickly, you said."

Maitland nodded. "He does sir. Quicker than anyone I've seen."

Stanton shrugged slightly. "Well, all we can do is try. If he says no, we'll find someone else."

Stanton rose. "Fields, your sentence is suspended due to the requirements of the service. I want you to come with me."

"Yes sir." I was confused. Nothing these men had said, or the questions they'd asked, made any sense. I was relieved I wasn't going to be punished, but at least punishment was predictable. This was impossible to understand.

"Confused, Private Fields?" Stanton reached for his hat.

"Yes sir."

"Well, you shouldn't be." He turned to me. "It's all very simple, really.

"You're going to meet General Brock."

8

"Do you know what a batman is, private?"

Stanton and I marched across the parade grounds to the garrison gate. "No sir."

"A batman is the personal assistant to an officer. A servant, really. He cleans the officer's boots, lays out his uniform, cares for his equipment, fetches him whatever needs fetching. Do you understand?"

"Yes sir," I lied.

"General Brock's batman died last year. The general was very fond of him. Porter had been the general's servant for years, ever since the general was in the West Indies. He has had no batman since."

We walked out the front gate of the fort and west to a small creek with a bridge. On the other side, I knew, was Government House, where Brock stayed.

"The general is now both commander of all forces in Upper Canada and president of the council," Stanton continued. "That means he is both the military and political head of this colony. Which is a rather large job."

"Yes sir."

"The general has decided—reluctantly—that he requires a new batman until this war is over. He asked me to choose one for him from the ranks. I have chosen you. What do you think?"

I didn't know what I thought. "Why me, sir?" I asked.

"Why indeed," he replied. "I'm not sure why. You're far too young, really, and not much of a conversationalist. Why *did* I pick you?"

He stopped, put his hands on his hips, and stared at me. "I picked you because you remind me of what I like best about the people here," he said finally. "You don't say much, you don't ask for much, but you're proud just the same, and stubborn. The best among you have those qualities. I admire them. I think the general does, too."

He shrugged. "At any rate, we'll soon see."

We walked in silence. I don't know what Stanton was thinking. I was trying not to think. I had gotten into a fight, and as a result I was being taken to General Brock to see if he wanted me as his batman. It made no sense.

It made even less sense because I noticed when I picked up my kit that the blanket was in it. I'd put it in there when I got up this morning, and forgotten. All the times MacPherson deserved a bloody nose, and I'd given him one when he was innocent. . . .

We arrived at Government House. It looked a bit like a very large barracks. The building was all one storey, in the shape of a U, with wood clapboarding on the outside—no fancy stone. There were lots of windows and chimneys, and a verandah, but it looked more like a soldier's house than a politician's.

A sentry at the front door saluted Stanton.

Stanton returned the salute. "Captain Stanton to speak to the general's orderly."

"One moment, sir." The sentry turned and rapped on the front door. The door opened, and an officer stepped outside, a thin and gloomy little man. For a moment I thought this was General Brock, but he was only an aide.

Stanton saluted. "Captain William Stanton, to speak with General Brock."

The orderly nodded and disappeared. A few moments later he returned. "The general will see you."

Stanton nodded and stepped inside, motioning me to follow.

We were in a hallway. Wood panelling lined the walls partway, with dark blue wallpaper covering the rest. Candles flickered from their holders on the walls. It was a rare thing for me to see candles—they were too expensive for most farmers. We'd always used a lamp with fat in it, or just relied on a fire.

"The general is in the library." The orderly nodded toward one of the closed doors.

"Thank you." Stanton turned to me. "Wait here."

He stepped to the door and knocked gently. A voice from inside told him to come in. Stanton opened the door, gave me a quick smile, then disappeared inside.

The orderly and I stood there, not looking at each other. I could feel his disapproval of me—one brief glance at my private's uniform said everything he wanted to know. I ignored him, and tried to make out the conversation going on inside. Their voices were muffled, but by listening hard I was able to catch the odd word or two.

" . . . Just a boy? . . . "

" . . . Quite clever, sir . . . "

" . . . I'm not sure I need . . . "

" . . . You had asked, sir . . ."

" . . . But a mere boy . . ."

The library door slid open and Stanton appeared. "Come in, Private Fields."

I took a breath, held it, and stepped into a room full of old books and rich furniture. A man in a crimson coat and white trousers stood by the fireplace holding a sheet of paper. He turned to look at me, and I looked at him.

He was tall, well over six feet, and broad, though not fat. His face was wide, with a strong jaw and a firm mouth. But his fine, blond hair and pale skin made him seem almost delicate.

I'd seen officers, of course, but not like this. Gold epaulettes glinted on his shoulders, his white shirt was ruffled and rich-looking, his boots were jet black. He was a gentleman.

I'm not sure I noticed all this at once. I do remember being overwhelmed by him. He was so clearly a powerful man, a man used to power.

"I suppose I should have got him to comb his hair," Stanton smiled apologetically.

"It doesn't matter." Brock's voice was quiet and smooth, but not soft. It reminded me of Stanton's voice, the voice people get when they have education and influence.

He stepped forward. "Captain Stanton is an officer with a singular talent for knowing good men from bad, and he thinks you are a good man. What do you think?"

I flushed. My mouth opened and closed, but nothing came out.

"Do you think you are a good man, Private Fields."

"I . . . I don't know, sir."

He frowned. "You don't know if you're good?"

I was lost, helpless. "I . . . I don't know, sir. I hope I'm good enough."

"Well," he smiled, "an honest answer. You said you're eighteen."

"Yes sir."

"Is that true?"

Lying seemed impossible in front of this man. "No sir."

"How old are you?"

"Almost sixteen, sir."

"Almost sixteen." He turned to Stanton. "He shouldn't even be in the army."

"No sir," Stanton agreed. "But he seemed better off with us than where we found him. He has acquitted himself well in training."

The general folded his arms and shook his head. "I don't know, Stanton."

Suddenly I resented this man. It was a ridiculous feeling, but I resented him. Who were these people, to stand over me as though I were some piece of livestock, to be bought and slaughtered?

I raised my head and looked at him. He seemed startled. We stared at each other for a second. I forced myself not to look away.

Finally he turned to Stanton. "If you think so, we'll try. Thank you, Stanton."

Stanton stiffened. "Very good, sir." He picked up his hat, marched to the door. "Good night, sir."

"Good night, Stanton."

Stanton shot me a parting look. I think he winked.

And then I was alone with Brock.

"We'll go into your duties in the morning. For now, you'll sleep in the kitchen. It's getting on, you'll probably want to sleep. Thompson!"

The orderly appeared in the doorway. "Sir."

"Look after the boy. He is to be my new batman."

The orderly's eyes widened momentarily. "Your batman, sir?"

Brock's face clouded. "That is what I said. Make a bed for him in the kitchen."

The orderly nodded. "Very good, sir."

"That will be all, Fields."

"Yes sir." I saluted.

"You don't need to salute me inside the house."

"Yes sir."

I followed Thompson down a long hall to a large kitchen. He disappeared, then returned with a straw mattress and some blankets. He threw them in a far corner of the kitchen, by the back door, then wheeled about and left.

I pulled the blankets over the mattress, blew out the candle on the table, and lay down. Sleep was impossible, but there was nothing else to do but try.

What had I gotten into? I was to serve this man, the general of all the troops in the army? How?

I thought of the farm. I belonged there. That's where I was born, and I should never have left. No matter what

Uncle Will had done, at least I knew him. I didn't know this man.

For the first time since I joined the army I felt homesick. Great waves of it washed over me. I found myself crying, and couldn't even remember when it started.

Figures moved about the house. Doors were closed, the light in the hallway went out. Things became quiet. I hoped no one could hear me.

Maybe an hour passed, maybe two. I lay on my back, staring at the ceiling. I thought about running away, going back home. But that would be deserting. They shot you for that.

I couldn't run away. I'd made decisions. All of them bad, all of them wrong, but I was stuck with it.

A bell rang in the kitchen. I jumped up. It rang again. What was I supposed to do? It must be the general wanting something, but what did he want? Did he want me? Where was he?

I scrambled out of bed. The bell rang again. I stumbled down the hallway to the front entrance. Everything was dark. The general must be in the other wing. I groped along the hall, then turned right, down another hall. It seemed to go on forever.

At the far end I saw a light, glowing from the bottom of a door. I walked toward it, tripped over a table and stubbed my toe, groaned to myself, and got the table right-side-up again.

At the door I paused. This wasn't right. Maybe the bell was for someone else. Maybe I should already have done something.

There was only one way to find out. I knocked.

"Come."

I opened the door and stepped inside. Brock was seated at a small table, writing on a sheet of parchment. His coat was off and he looked almost like an average person.

He looked up. "Ah, Fields, good. I'm rather hungry. There should be some cold roast beef in the pantry. Fix me a sandwich and a glass of beer." He returned to his writing.

I stepped back out of the room, then cursed myself for forgetting to salute or say "Yes sir." But then, he said I didn't have to salute. But surely you should *say* something.

I hurried back to the kitchen. How did you light the candles? Where were the matches? Ah, there. Now the pantry. Is that the pantry? Yes. And there's the roast beef. And bread. Now . . . how do you make a sandwich?

I'd never eaten a sandwich, and certainly never made one. At home we ate our meat with the bread on the side. I knew that in a sandwich the meat went in between two slices of bread. How do you cut the meat?

Get a knife. Right. Now, cut off a hunk of the beef. Like so. Now the bread. Good. Put the beef on one slice, put the other slice on top. Good. That looks like a sandwich.

Now the beer. Where is it? There it is. Damn! Never mind, clean it up later.

I put the sandwich on a plate and, balancing plate and glass, navigated back along the hall, and then down the other hall. I couldn't knock, but the door was ajar, so I pushed it open with my foot.

"Your sandwich, sir."

"Ah, good." Brock leaned back and stretched. "Put it here."

I set the sandwich and beer on the table. He looked at the sandwich, raised the top piece of bread, lowered it, and looked at me.

"Have you ever made a sandwich before, Fields?"

"No, sir."

Maybe it was better like this. Instant disgrace. I'd get a whipping, be sent back to my barracks, and this nightmare would be over.

Brock stood up. "Follow me."

I followed him all the way back to the kitchen. He went to the pantry, took out the bread and roast beef.

"I am going to teach you how to make a sandwich. Please observe. First I sharpen the knife on the stone, like this. Then I cut the bread, thinly. It is important that it be thin. Now I apply butter to one piece of the bread. I spread it like so. Then I slice the beef. Again, thinly. Then I place the beef on the unbuttered piece of bread. Then I take the horseradish. Have you ever had horseradish, Fields? It's quite delicious on beef. I spread the horseradish over the beef, like so. Then I place the buttered piece of bread over the beef.

"That, Fields, is a sandwich." He took a large bite, chewed it several times, swallowed, and sighed.

"Go back to bed, Fields. We'll continue your education in the morning." Carrying his sandwich, he disappeared down the hall.

I cleaned up the spilled beer, then got back into bed. He hadn't seemed angry. It almost seemed as though he enjoyed the whole thing. The general in charge of all Upper Canada had just taught me how to make a sandwich.

It was too much to understand. I went to sleep.

9

The next month was the most frightening I'd ever spent. There were a thousand things to know, and I didn't know one of them.

I didn't know how to rub grease into fine leather to make it soft and rich, or starch a shirt until it crackled when you unfolded it.

I couldn't saddle a horse. I couldn't prepare a bottle of wine for drinking—removing the cork, pouring the wine into a decanter, letting it sit for the proper length of time. I'd never even tasted wine.

All these things and a thousand more I couldn't do but had to do, if I was to be a general's batman.

So why didn't Brock get rid of me? Why didn't he send me back to my barracks and have me replaced with someone who knew *something*, at least, about how a general's batman behaves?

I'm not sure of the answer, but I have an idea. For one thing, I learned quick. I didn't know much, but there wasn't much I had to be told twice. Although most of the staff ignored me, there was a maid there, Maggie, who seemed to like me. She showed me how to cook and sew and take grass stains out of white trousers.

"Just be patient," she told me once, when I fumed at not being able to make the general's brass buttons shine. "You're learning, and as long as you're learning he'll put up with you."

He put up with an awful lot. Like the morning I prepared his bath and forgot to add the cold water. He stepped in, let out a howl that would send a regiment into retreat, and came storming into the hall stark naked.

"I wanted to be bathed, not poached!" he shouted, and disappeared back inside.

Maggie showed me how to draw a proper bath.

And there was the day I cinched the general's saddle wrong and he solemnly slid off the back end of his horse, saddle and all. I was sure that was the end.

But he just showed me how to properly saddle a horse.

It was as though he liked to show me things. He taught me a lot about horses. Alfred was his horse—a big grey stallion that he'd had for years. He showed me how to feed him, and clean out his stable, and groom him and comb his mane.

A lot of people thought it was strange that a general who should be preparing for war was spending time showing a boy how to care for a horse. But I think he wanted to do it. He worked late into every night on papers and letters and maps, and he was up every morning before dawn. I think showing me how to do simple things relaxed him, helped him not to think too much.

He also decided to educate me. Mostly this meant correcting how I spoke. He complained that I never said my "g's" in words like "cleaning" or "thinking," and that my subjects never agreed with my verbs, whatever that meant.

"You were born with the accent of your people, and sadly there's nothing we can do about it," he told me once. "But we do not have to tolerate that accent *and* shoddy speech as well."

It was frightening, but it was exciting too. I was learning things—things I'd never learned on the farm, and never would have learned. Brock lived in a different world from mine, a world of officers and politicians and rich folk, where people were polite and ate fine food and talked about serious things as though they were unimportant, and unimportant things as though they were serious. I thought of my cousin Seth. *He'd* never learn how to decant a bottle of claret. It made me feel superior.

I also spent a lot of time travelling. With the outbreak of war most of the troops in the garrison had been sent to the Niagara frontier. Brock often sailed across the end of the lake to Fort George to supervise the defences. Whenever he went, I went with him. The first time I sailed in the tiny ship my stomach felt like glass, but after that things got better. I started to look forward to the trips.

When Brock was in York he would meet with local politicians and militia officers. The militia were local civilians who were given some training in soldiering and then told to stand ready in case a battle was coming up. But many of the militia seemed unwilling to mobilize. There were crops to attend to, and families to protect. No one was really certain how many could be counted on if it came to a battle.

But without more troops, how could Brock defend Upper Canada? The British had only 1,200 soldiers in uniform to defend a colony that stretched from Fort Malden in the west to Lake Superior in the North to the Ottawa River in the east. There were other troops in Lower Canada, but the Governor General—Brock's superior—was in Quebec and wanted an army kept there.

It should have been hopeless, and many people said it was. But rumour had it the Americans were having trouble with their soldiers, too. Farmers there didn't seem any more eager to go off to war than we did. Troops were complaining about bad food, bare feet, and no pay. It sounded familiar.

Still, the Yankees had put together two armies, each one larger than all the British regulars put together. One had reached Detroit, and was preparing to cross the river to the Canadian side. The other was gathering on the Niagara River, and would be ready to cross, the officers figured, at any time.

I think I knew more about what was going on than most soldiers. I could hear conversations coming through doors. It seemed to me things were coming to a head. I kept my mouth shut.

It was a grey morning in late July when the soldier, as

exhausted as the horse under him, rode up to Government House and demanded to see General Brock. Brock was shaving, but when he heard the message he came bounding to the front door, his face still half-covered in soap.

"Are you from Amherstburg?"

"Yes sir. I have a message from Colonel St. George at Fort Malden."

Brock tore open the envelope and began to read. The news was bad. You could tell when the news was bad by his face, which became frozen, expressionless, as though he was afraid of betraying his feelings.

"Fields." He wheeled around to where I was standing. "Go to the garrison. See if Colonel Procter has arrived yet from Fort George. If he has, ask him to come here immediately."

I rushed to the garrison. Procter was pouring water over his head to wash off the dust of the ride from Fort George when I burst in with the message. Procter stared, then stalked out of the room without bothering to dry himself and called for his horse.

When I got back to Government House Procter and Brock were already in the library, talking. They'd forgotten to close the door completely. It was my duty to stand outside the door in case I was needed, so there was no way I could keep from overhearing. I strained to catch every word.

Brock was speaking. "The Americans have crossed the Detroit River and are encamped at Sandwich. We can expect an attack on Fort Malden any day."

For a moment Procter was silent. Finally he spoke up.

"Sir, can Fort Malden resist?"

Someone in the room was pacing. It had to be Brock. "Colonel St. George doesn't think they can. He has only two hundred regular troops against an invading army of two thousand. The local militia seems reluctant to fight—they're desperate to return to their farms. Many are deserting. The Indians are accusing our soldiers of giving up before the battle. They may be right."

"Can we get reinforcements to them?"

"From where? Their army on the Niagara could strike us at any time. And we receive no reinforcements from Quebec. Governor-General Prevost refuses to send more men while there is a chance of ending the war by negotiation. He fears 'provoking' the Americans. Since they have invaded Upper Canada, I would say they are already provoked."

"Sir." Procter's voice was eager, even excited. "If we can turn the Americans back at Amherstburg it will be a great blow against them. Their volunteers will abandon their army. And the Americans might decide we're too strong for an attack across the Niagara."

"I agree." This was Brock again. "We cannot afford to lose Amherstburg. If we do we will have armies against our back as well our front. But without more men, how can I?"

"It could already be too late." Procter's mood became gloomy. "By the time our troops arrive, Fort Malden could have fallen."

"Nevertheless, we must act." I could imagine Brock running his hand through his hair. It was a habit with him when he was thinking hard.

"We will detach part of our force at Fort George on the Niagara, and send it to Fort Erie. It, at least, is closer to Detroit. The men there can reach either battle in time if they must.

"We will also send several detachments down the valley of the Thames River. They will recruit as many militia as they can and be ready to repel the Americans, should they attempt to push eastward."

He paused for a moment. "Colonel Procter."

"Sir."

"If it were my choice, I would leave for Amherstburg myself in the morning. But for now I must stay here. I am sending you to Amherstburg in my place, to relieve Colonel St. George. He is an able commander, but a cautious one. This is no time for caution."

"I am honoured, sir."

"Honour us all, Colonel, with a victory."

Procter's face when he left the library was sombre. But the minute he was out the front door he raced toward his horse.

Brock came out of the library. "Fields." He motioned me toward him.

"Sir."

"Pack a light kit for me. Two uniforms, other necessary clothing, and toiletries—three weeks' worth."

"Yes sir."

"Pack a kit for yourself," Brock added. "And be ready with food for the both of us." He turned, then paused and looked back at me. "Be very sure everything is ready for us to depart at any time. One way or another, we shall be leaving this house soon."

"Yes sir."

He disappeared down the hall.

I set to work, with Maggie's help. She made me pack, unpack, and repack the trunk over and over, "until you can do it in your sleep," she said. I soon knew every item in that trunk like it was my own.

Brock was up even later that night. I stayed awake too, and brought him a sandwich at midnight, though he didn't ask for it. Sometimes, I noticed, he forgot he was hungry.

He was happy to see the sandwich. The general loved roast beef with horseradish. "All packed?" he asked.

"Yes sir. The trunk is in the closet in the main hall."

"I'll look at it in the morning. That's all, Fields."

I stepped back to the door.

"Fields." He turned in his chair. "Let me ask you a question."

"Yes sir?"

"If a large animal, let us say a moose, appeared in the woods in front of you, how would you protect yourself?"

I gazed at him blankly. "Sir?"

"How would you protect yourself?" he repeated. "Would you run at him and try to frighten him off, or escape up a tree?"

I had no idea what he was talking about. Why did he want to know about a moose?

But he'd asked a question, and he was a general, and I had to give an answer.

I thought for a moment. "I guess . . . I guess I would run at him sir. But I'd size up the nearest tree while I was doin' it."

" 'Do-*ing*,' Fields."

"Do-*ing*, sir."

He nodded. "Thank you. Good night, Fields."

"Good night, sir."

I left him and went to my bed in the kitchen, to lie awake and wonder why a general would be interested in a moose.

10

The next two weeks seemed like a constant rush toward doing nothing. Brock returned to Fort George, and then came back again to Fort York. He spent endless hours with officers and merchants and politicians, meeting and organizing.

But despite all the talk no one seemed to know what was going to happen. Two Yankee armies were on our doorstep. We probably didn't have enough men to beat even one of them. We certainly didn't have enough men to fight both. Everyone said Fort Malden was finished. Most predicted Fort George would be next.

Everyone was waiting—for the Yankees to take Amherstburg, for the invasion at Niagara to begin, for the final battle. Not many people doubted how the battle would end.

But I became convinced everyone was wrong. Brock was building to something. I didn't know what. But each day he seemed more determined to . . . to what? He had an idea. I couldn't tell you what it was, but it had formed in his mind. He would pause halfway to where he was going, and just stare ahead, frozen motionless, maybe for a minute. Then he would shake his head, mutter something, and go on.

I didn't know what his plan was, but it was coming together in moments like that. He couldn't see it himself perhaps, not fully. But once it was formed, he would act.

How could I know this? I was just a servant, after all, in charge of running errands and pressing clothes and making roast beef sandwiches. I was the last person in the world to make predictions about this war.

But I was getting to know Brock, maybe better than some others knew him. He was a distant man, reserved with his officers and men, positively cold to civilians. I don't think he had a single friend. I don't think he'd ever had one.

But I saw him at night, when everyone else was in bed and he was alone in his study. Once I arrived with food he didn't know he wanted. I found him walking around a map, around and around, studying it from every angle. Suddenly he plunged at it, stabbed a finger at the middle and practically shouted, "There!" At that moment I felt certain a battle was about to be won.

I caught glimpses of him—the way he would arrange his face the second before he stepped into a room to greet people, the way he would stop in mid-stride to watch a robin wrestle a worm out of the ground, as if the robin—or maybe the worm—held the secret to the war, the way he would ask Maggie if her daughter was over the croup and listen gravely while Maggie explained how you dealt with a sick child.

One morning, while I was in the kitchen pressing his

uniform, he suddenly wandered in and sat down at the table. I asked him if he needed anything, but he just waved me away—"No, no, carry on." So I went on pressing his coat, while he looked out the window at the clothes flapping on the line in the morning breeze.

"Jeremy?" he said suddenly. "How did you get here?"

"Sir?"

"How did you get into the army? Do your parents know you're here?"

"My parents are dead, sir."

"I'm sorry." There was no false grief in it, just a sort of acknowledgement.

"I left the farm after my mother died, and walked here."

"Did you want to become a soldier?"

"No sir. I just wanted to see things. When Captain Stanton came along, I decided to join up."

He leaned back in the kitchen chair and studied me. "Why didn't you stay on the farm?" he asked.

I thought for a moment, and then answered with the truth. "I'm not a farmer, sir."

He considered this for a moment. "No," he said finally, "I don't think you would make a good farmer. I must say, though, you have become a rather good batman."

My face flushed. "Thank you, sir."

"Watch how you press that collar."

"Yes sir."

And he left. If I'd known a hymn, I'd have sung it.

August fifth dawned grey and rainy. I was up with the sun,

but when I went to Brock's room he was already dressed and at work. I brought him some breakfast and a pot of coffee and got out of his way. He seemed different this morning, even more intense.

Shortly after nine he came bounding out of his room, shouting my name. I ran out from the kitchen and met him at the front door.

"Sir?"

He handed me a note. "Fields, go to the garrison and give this message to Major Watson. Then come back here and make sure my kit is ready to be loaded onto a wagon. See to it you're packed as well."

Before I could even reply he was out the door and on his horse.

I sprinted from Government House to the garrison. Major Watson was still finishing his breakfast when I reached the officer's mess, panting. He read the note with his mouth full of bacon and eggs. Suddenly he stopped chewing and swallowed hard.

"Cheevers!"

A young officer ran up. "Sir!"

"Take three men. Find the commanders of the militia and have them report here immediately. And muster the men. Have them ready to march on an hour's notice."

"Yes, *sir.*"

Weeks we had spent waiting, drilling, doing nothing. Now, in an instant, everything was action. Soldiers ran from one place to another. Even officers half-jogged. Horses and mules were hitched to wagons. Men with lists called out numbers, while other men counted sacks of things and

shouted numbers back. It looked like complete confusion
—to anyone who wasn't a soldier.

I didn't have much time to watch. I went back to
Government House and unpacked and repacked the trunk
one more time. Then I went to Brock's bedroom. He had
already packed a smaller trunk beside his bed with maps
and papers and a set of pistols. I dragged it downstairs, and
loaded it and the big trunk onto a wagon that had been
brought around. Brock had left more instructions. He
wanted a small table, chair, and cot loaded into the wagon
as well. We would find them in the attic.

Brock was at the legislature. He sent a note ordering all
militia and garrison officers to a counsel at Government
House at two in the afternoon. Most arrived early. They
paced about, looked at each other, sent off notes to their
troops, and paced some more.

Brock was late getting back. He strode through the front
door and into the library, motioning the other officers to
follow. No one even thought to close the door. I took up my
station outside, ready and listening.

Brock wasted no time. "I have prorogued the legislature." He paused a moment, to let it sink in. I wasn't sure
what it meant, but it sounded serious.

"Since the civilian government is now temporarily suspended," Brock continued, "there is no need for me to
attend to its needs. I have decided to move into the field.
We are going to engage the enemy."

Someone muttered, "Here, here." The rest were silent.
There had been rumours that not all the officers were as
eager to fight as Brock was.

"Do you plan to relieve Amherstburg, sir, or concentrate on the Niagara front?" one of them asked.

"Both."

"But sir—"

"Here is what I intend to do. Gentlemen, if you will look at this map." Brock had made up his mind.

"I plan to leave this evening for Port Dover. I have already sent word for the Norfolk militia to be ready for us when we arrive."

An older man, with an accent like my own, spoke gravely. "If the Norfolk militia is to march with you sir, the York militia will not be denied."

The news clearly pleased Brock. "It gladdens my heart to hear it, sir. Very well, then. My plans are to leave this evening by boat for Burlington Bay. I will take one hundred of the York militia with me. From Burlington Bay we will march to Dover, then sail to Amherstburg."

"But sir," one of them interrupted. "If the Americans attack at Niagara, you will be hundreds of miles away."

"I do not believe the Americans are ready to attack. They are as cautious there as in Detroit—everything must be perfect, the gods themselves must be visibly smiling, before they will move. We still have time.

"As soon as we arrive at Amherstburg, I plan to combine our troops with the troops and Indians now there and attack the American army. Once it is defeated we will rush the troops back to Niagara, to be ready for the American attack there.

"Well gentlemen, any questions?"

For a while there was only silence. No one seemed to

know what to say. Finally, someone spoke up. I thought I noticed a slight tremble in his voice.

"Sir, the Americans have more than two thousand troops in Detroit now. Even if the militia turns out and the Indians agree to fight, you will have barely half that. Surely we can only hope for victory by taking a defensive stance."

"We have no time for defence. We must attack before the Americans realize what we've done."

There was silence again. Even without being able to see them I could feel the doubt in the room. They didn't believe in their general's plan.

Brock knew it too. "I understand your concern," he said. "We are taking a considerable risk. But we must take risks if we are to have even a hope of success. And I believe this plan will succeed.

"Gentlemen, I have studied my enemy. I know the generals who command the Yankee armies. I have never met them, but I have gone over every battle they have fought, and they are both weak. Their General Hull, in Detroit, has had a week to attack Amherstburg, and he has not. Why? Because he is a timid man, and will not attack unless he can be certain, absolutely *certain*, of success. I would have thought success at Amherstburg would be as certain as one could hope for, but it seems it is not certain enough for General Hull.

"The commander in the east, General Dearborn, is no better. Did you know he is so fat that he has to be lifted onto his horse? Fat generals are bad generals, gentlemen. They do not seize the moment. They are too busy getting onto their horses.

"And it seems certain now that we can count on the support of the Indian nations. The Shawnee leader Tecumseh has formed a large confederation, including the Wyandot, the Delaware, the Kickapoo, the Potawatomi, the Lake Indians, and others. The Americans are terrified that if they lose a battle the Indians will show no mercy.

"So. I believe the Americans will not attack Niagara, just as they have not attacked Amherstburg. They fear the consequences of battle. And armies that are full of fear can never gain victory."

And that was that. There were more orders, more consultations, but the decision had been made. Brock had made it. There was nothing to do now but obey.

The officers left Government House shaking their heads and muttering. But once out the door they practically broke into a run. There was much to do. They only had hours to get ready. These men may not have believed in Brock's plan, but they'd agreed to follow him, and there was nothing for it but to prepare.

I was kept busy running messages, and in between stuffing as much food into a satchel as I could. I had no idea what we would be eating during the trip, and I wanted the general to enjoy Maggie's cooking for as long as possible.

It was early evening when Brock rode up on Alfred. I was in the wagon, securing the trunks. He took a quick look at the luggage, and nodded his head in satisfaction.

"Look after my trunks, Fields. I will win the war, if you will not lose my kit."

"I won't sir."

He galloped off toward the garrison, and we slowly

followed. Already the volunteer troops were streaming into the garrison and organizing themselves at the docks. A schooner rested at anchor, ready to sail. The men and supplies rowed out on boats. It seemed to take forever—getting Alfred to stand quietly on a barge during the ride out to the schooner was especially exciting—but it wasn't even midnight when the last of us clambered on deck.

The night was dark, the stars hidden by clouds. A fine mist wet the skin and soaked through the clothes. The sailors scrambled up the masts and unfurled the sails. I stood amidships and looked back to see Brock standing on the deck above me, staring hard into the night.

The wind caught the sails. The ship shuddered forward.

We were on our way to war.

We sailed through the night, reaching the harbour of Burlington Bay as the sun rose from the flat waters of Lake Ontario. It took several hours to unload the boats and form up the men, but by noon we were on our way again.

Now that we were finally on the move, every hour seemed to count. We marched at a quick step, and men who had never marched behind anything except a plough sweated and cursed the heavy kits on their backs. Every now and then Brock would leave the front of the column and ride down the line, examining the troops, calling for the men to close up, encouraging an exhausted soldier, reprimanding a sloppy sergeant. It seemed to help.

The sun was low in the sky when we made camp outside a little village called Ancaster. Word came that I was to take the wagon to the general's tent, in the middle of the camp. The driver manoeuvred us through the instant city of canvas being thrown up, and I found Brock pacing about impatiently.

"I was wondering where you'd got to," he snapped. "I need another uniform, and this one must be cleaned."

I hurriedly unpacked his clothes and set to work with a damp sponge at getting the dust off his uniform. (Maggie had shown me how.) I was polishing his sword when he emerged from his tent.

"Never mind that, Fields." He took his sword from my hands. "Go into the village and find some place with wine and cheese and bread. I will ride into the village in an hour. Have it ready for me then."

"Sir." I scurried away toward the village, then wondered how I would find wine and cheese and bread without any money. It was too late to ask. I continued on.

The village was packed with people. Dozens of men and women walked up and down its street, mostly in pairs. Little knots of half a dozen or so would form, then dissolve, then re-form. When I found the inn it was just as crowded. I had to squeeze through the men who gathered around the tables.

The talk was about war. Riders from our column had spread out and ahead of us, calling the militia to arms and to meet here. Most of them had just arrived.

There was plenty of argument. Many of these men wanted to fight. The people around here were the descendents of Loyalists, and they had no wish to become Yankees again.

But the winter wheat was ripe and ready to harvest. This was no time to be leaving a farm. What would their wives do? The men argued back and forth among themselves, lowering their voices only when one of them noticed my uniform.

I reached the bar, but had trouble getting anyone's attention. Finally I shouted at a big, fat man who stood at the end and looked to be the owner. He scowled at me.

"What do you want, boy?"

I stiffened. "I am batman to General Brock. He sends his compliments, and requests the honour of your hospitality in the form of a light supper of wine and cheese and bread."

Brock had taught me to talk like that when doing official things. I still wasn't very good at it. Other officers usually smiled when I tried.

But the fat man was impressed. "Pleased, I'm sure, to serve His Excellency," he gushed. "Will His Excellency be dining here?"

"No. He asks that I bring the supper to him. He is to arrive within the hour."

But I was wrong. Minutes later there was a commotion outside and someone shouted, "There he is!" The inn emptied. I grabbed the food from the startled fat man and rushed outside. I didn't bother to ask how much it cost.

Brock and several officers were talking with some important-looking men at one end of the street. I pushed through the crowd forming around them, and reached the general just as a tall man in a tall hat began addressing the crowd.

"Fellow citizens, I beg your attention. . . ."

He was someone important in the village, which gave him the right to launch into a long speech. I caught Brock's eye, and raised the covered plate of food and flask of wine. He nodded his head to the side of the crowd. When I got there he stepped away from the soldiers and the speaker and took the plate. It was dark by now—the only light came from two torches behind the important man. Most people there never knew the commander of all British forces in Upper Canada ate his supper standing up while they listened to a speech.

The timing was good—Brock was just finishing the last of the cheese when the fellow reached the end.

". . . With the love of our King in our hearts and the strength of righteousness in our arms, we shall preserve our glorious land and repel the alien invaders. God save the King!"

There was some polite applause, but little more. The men in the crowd knew the British were here to ask them to march away to war. They weren't at all sure they wanted to go. But they'd been promised that Brock would talk to them about his plans, and they had come to hear Brock. The other speeches were just something to put up with.

The important man then introduced Brock, telling them the general needed no introduction, and then spent so much time introducing him anyway that Brock was able to finish off the wine. The introduction probably would have gone on longer, except that Brock stepped back into the light of the torches, and the important man's remarks were drowned in a chorus of "Let him speak!" "Let the general speak!"

The man gave up and moved back, motioning Brock to take his place in the circle of light. Brock stepped forward, cleared his throat (a bit of bread caught in the gullet, maybe), put his hand on the handle of his sword, and began to talk.

He spoke quietly, without fancy words. He would have

been impossible to hear, except for the dead silence that filled the street.

"Gentlemen, ladies, I am grateful you are here tonight. My purpose in asking you here is to tell you of your government's plans to repel the American invaders, and to call for the militia to fight."

He outlined the plan of the campaign. He left nothing out—if an American spy were in the crowd, the enemy would have known everything.

But the crowd knew that too. They realized that Brock was showing how much he trusted them.

". . . Many of you are the descendents of those who came to this colony because of their loyalty to Great Britain. Many others are the descendents of British veterans who were given land in reward for their services to the King. Now *you*, gentlemen, are being called upon. I cannot promise you an easy time. There will be fighting. You will be away from your homes and fields until the snow arrives. It will be difficult for you and your families."

He gazed at the dark faces that gazed back at him from the shadows outside the light. Were they loyal? Would they follow him?

". . . It will be difficult, but I believe the end will justify the difficulty. For I believe we shall defeat the invading armies. I cannot promise that we will. I can only promise you that I will give everything, even my life if need be, to protect you from your enemies and preserve this colony for your descendents and for the Empire."

And that was it. He turned, nodded to his men, and stepped out of the light. But not before someone shouted,

"God save General Brock!" and the cry was taken up by every voice on the street.

"God save General Brock!"

"God save the King!"

"God save Upper Canada!"

Brock mounted Alfred and, nodding to the cheering crowd, disappeared into the darkness.

I made my way back to the camp, to Brock's tent. He didn't want anything, ignored me really. He was bent over his maps again, measuring distances by the light of a sputtering candle. I found him a better candle, then retreated to the wagon a few feet away.

I'd fallen asleep by the time the officers arrived, but I was soon awake and listening.

"... Astonishing, sir. More than two hundred men have asked to join us, and we hear that more are proceeding directly to Port Dover. Sir, we won't have enough room in the boats. What are we going to do with them?"

"Bless them," he said finally. "Bless them all. Well, pick the men you feel are best able to endure the campaign, and have them ready to march with us at dawn."

All through the next day we marched farther south and farther west. There was something thrilling in the air. After all the months of waiting, now we were going to fight. The men sang songs as they marched. I'd never really sung before, but I found I liked it. All the while men kept appearing, muskets in hand, asking if they could join the fight. If we'd had more boats at Dover, we could have sent Amherstburg a thousand men.

It was late afternoon of our second day of marching

when we reached Lake Erie. Brock had already ridden ahead. As we approached the beach I could see him marching up and down along the shoreline, stopping every now and then to wave his arms at a collection of wooden boats hauled up along the sand.

By now I knew the routine. I threaded the wagon through the encamping troops until I reached the spot in the middle where they always put Brock's tent. I moved the small table, the chair and the cot inside, then got someone to help me with the trunk. Then I raced over to the canteen where they were already at work on supper, and made sure the general's meal was being looked after. When it was cooked, I took it back to the tent, and let it warm over the nearest fire.

Brock came stalking toward his tent about an hour later. He was accompanied by some officers and a man in a rough woollen outfit with a battered cap plastered to his head. The man's face was pale as soap, and it seemed to get paler the more Brock spoke.

"This is intolerable." Brock grabbed his supper from me, and for a moment I thought he was complaining about the food. But it was the pale-faced man who was getting the general's abuse.

"This is absolutely intolerable. There are not nearly enough boats here to move this army. I may have to leave half the men here on the beach. You could have cost us this war, you fool!"

"But general—"

"And what boats there are aren't seaworthy. Most of them would sink before we were out of sight of this beach.

You would make me the only general in history who *drowned* his army!"

"Sir, if you would only—"

"We will have to delay. We will have to spend all of tonight caulking and repairing the boats. Every man will have to work at it."

"Sir, there are local men who can repair—"

"Then get them here! Tell them we will do everything we can to assist. If a shipwright has an order for me, *I* will serve him!"

"Sir, I truly believe—"

"Why are you standing here? Didn't you hear my orders? Get to it. All of you!"

"Sir!"

That night I found myself with a brush in my hand, painting tar over the gaping seams of one of the boats. I had plenty of company—every man in the militia.

We were allowed only a couple of hours of rest, in shifts, and then we were called back to work. I was covered in a black, gooey mess of tar. It was all over my clothes and hands, and eventually my face. Every now and then the men would strip and throw themselves into the cold waves that rolled onto the beach. They would shiver and rub their skin, trying to get the tar off, but it never worked. They came back wet and miserable, and were sent straight back to work.

All that night and through the next day we were at it. My back ached from carrying endless buckets from huge caul-drons that ceaselessly bubbled with the filthy stuff. If I'd known any more, I might have worked on caulking the seams with pitch, just about as bad as tar, or nailing fresh wood into place where rotten planks had been before. But farm boys aren't sailors, and I did the worst jobs, because they were the only ones I could do.

Brock was around us constantly. He inspected every boat, over and over again, looking for flaws, encouraging the men. I don't think he slept at all. If he got food, it wasn't from me.

I groaned the next morning when the drums called us to rise and make ready. Brock was gone from his tent. I had already loaded the trunks and furniture onto one of the boats, and now it suddenly occurred to me that I might be left behind. We'd been told there was room for only 250 of the men in the boats; a hundred others were being sent back to their farms.

I raced down the beach, and found Brock giving orders about which companies were going in which boats. I asked a lieutenant what boat the general had assigned himself, and he impatiently pointed to the one at the western end of the beach. I trotted along until I found it—Brock had already had his small trunk moved there. I climbed in and perched myself on top.

The boats were packed, almost overflowing. Twenty-five men apiece shoved and jostled for space. Eight of them manned the four oars. In the middle of each boat a small sail hung from a mast. At the bow an officer stood ready, while at the stern whoever knew anything about sailing manned the rudder. Until we reached Detroit, he would be the one in charge; the officer was nothing more than an ornament.

Our boat was loaded and ready when Brock finally arrived with another officer. He started to climb in, then noticed me. "Fields, what are you doing here? I don't need you. I want you to return to Government House."

No! This was impossible! I couldn't get this far, and then be sent back.

It was strange. I shouldn't have cared. This war, this army, this man—they shouldn't mean that much. I hadn't wanted to become a soldier, it just happened. I hadn't wanted to serve Brock. Someone else had decided for me.

And the war? What did I care whose flag waved where?

But somehow, now, I was part of it. It's all anyone around me had thought about, talked about, for weeks. It was the reason we were here. I had to be part of it. I wanted to see how it turned out.

And I didn't want to leave Brock. I'd gotten used to looking after him. Looking after him was my job, and it was a good job.

"Sir—" I hesitated. "Sir, I want to go. Sir, you need me."

He raised an eyebrow. "I *need* you?"

"Yes sir. Without me . . . you'll forget to eat."

A laugh rippled through the men in the boat. Brock cleared his throat and it stopped.

"Well." I could have sworn I saw the ends of his mouth twitch, as though he were forcing back a smile. "We can hardly have the general starve, can we? I suppose you'd better come. But if we all drown, don't blame me."

"I won't, sir."

The men on the shore helped push the boats into the surf that rolled up onto the shallow beach. It seemed to take forever until the sand stopped scraping against the wooden hull and the boat floated free in the waves. There was a lot of shouting and swearing as the oarsmen tried to figure out how to make their boats work and those manning the rudders could manoeuvre their crafts into place.

But eventually we formed a ragged line. Slowly, we began to inch our way across the water. Our course was west, southwest.

Our next port of call: Amherstburg.

12

The rain returned, and it was cold and we were wet. It only took an hour on the water to convince me that the army was better than the navy.

We stayed within sight of shore. The boats were too small and too leaky to risk open water. The endless rolling lake stretching to the southern horizon made me feel glad the shore was near.

After about an hour the breeze picked up and we unfurled the sails. The oarsmen stopped rowing and we clipped along at a good pace.

The slowest vessel was a schooner called the *Chippawa*. It had been sent from Niagara to escort us, but mostly it just held us up. The wind was too light to fill her sails, and she limped along, the rest of us having to pause regularly to give her a chance to catch up. If it weren't for the fact that she was carrying a hundred troops from Fort Erie, we might have left her behind.

For a while things went well. We sailed west, the wind fair, the waves gentle. Except for the rain, I might have enjoyed it.

It was mid-afternoon when we came upon Long Point

peninsula. The narrow ridge of sand stretched out into the lake for miles. It would take hours to sail around it. The captain of the *Chippawa* said there was a channel through the peninsula that was sometimes deep enough for his ship to get through. We found the channel, and our boats made it fine, but the *Chippawa* struck bottom. We had to climb out of our boats into waist-deep water and pull the schooner through with ropes. It was exhausting, and we were already exhausted. No one had got any decent sleep in days.

Back in the boat, the wind fresher now and our pace faster, I found the lake taking hold of me. The great, gentle waves we rolled over were green and grey and edged with foam. I fell into some kind of trance watching them. Gulls screeched at us overhead. No one seemed to think much of gulls, but to me they were magnificent.

Brock ignored the gulls, ignored the water. He sat at the bow of the boat staring ahead, silent, as though if he thought hard enough he could push us to Amherstburg faster. What was happening there? Had the Americans attacked the fort? Had they captured it? Was there even any point to this mission? No one knew, not even Brock.

Late that day the sky grew darker and the clouds got lower, and the wind died. The captain of the *Chippawa* was certain a storm was approaching. We headed for an inlet, Brock scowling at the sky and the delay.

We hauled our boats onto shore, turned them over, and huddled underneath as the rain came lashing down, each man tight up against the other. We tried not to think of how miserable we felt.

Brock was wetter than any of us. He kept leaving our boat to walk along the beach, talking with the sentries, encouraging the men. The officers warned him he'd fall ill, but he ignored them.

The man was impossible to understand sometimes. In the boats he was impatient, brooding, silent. Now, stuck on the beach in the middle of a storm, he seemed cheerful, even excited.

"I would not have believed it," he whispered to an officer beside me in the middle of the night. "These men are soaked to the skin, exhausted. But their spirits are high. They're anxious to get on. I would have expected grumbling, calls to turn back. But every man seems determined to see this through."

"They want to fight, sir," the young officer replied. "The men are eager to fight."

"I wonder . . ." Brock stared out into the rainy darkness. "I wonder if the Americans are eager to fight?"

The next day was still cloudy, and colder now. The wind had a September bite to it, which cut through our wet clothes miserably. But within an hour of sunrise we were back on the water, cursing the wind and thinking about hot tea.

It was a mistake to curse the wind. Shortly before noon it died, and the life went out of the sails. Brock ordered us to the oars again, and we rowed. It was back-breaking work, and we crawled along. A soldier was only good on the oars for an hour at most, and then he had to be taken off and replaced. The troops were getting more and more tired, and we were still a long way from our destination. And a battle lay ahead.

Late that afternoon another storm came up. The boats

headed to shore again. Brock ground his fist into his palm when he gave the order.

The wind and rain lasted until almost midnight. Then suddenly, it stopped. A clear, fresh breeze took its place. The call from the officers echoed along the beach.

"Prepare the boats! Prepare to get under way!"

We were going to sail in the dark.

The fleet sailed in a column, led by a lantern hanging from the stern of the lead boat, our boat. I didn't like sailing in the dark. It was impossible to tell water from sky, up from down. I began to think about drowning, disappearing into dark waters, lost forever to light. I shook myself.

When we hit the rock I was sitting on Brock's trunk, and the impact sent me pitching forward. We were all entangled in each other's arms and legs, trying to get ourselves straightened out, frightened we were sinking.

"Steady on, men, the boat's all right." Brock's voice calmed things down. We had ridden up on the rock. There hadn't been much damage, but the problem now was to get off. The other boats following us were closing fast, probably wondering why the light from our lantern wasn't moving.

Suddenly Brock stood up, grabbed the side of the boat, and jumped overboard before anyone could even call out. There was a great splash, and then there he was beside us, up to his shoulders in water, pushing on the boat.

"Come on, men," he called out. "This is no place to get stuck."

Every man jumped out at once and started pushing. The boat was off the rock in less than a minute. We climbed back in, soaked and laughing.

"Carry on, Mr. Billings," Brock called out to the steersman. "And no more rocks, please."

The men shook their heads and laughed, as though their commander were some crazy relative they all loved anyway. I think the men had started to love Brock.

We reached Point Pelee that morning. Brock called the boats to shore. Many of the men dropped onto the sand and fell asleep where they were. Others made fires and boiled water for tea. We were only a few hours from Amherstburg. And we were weary to the bone.

The tea I was making for Brock was barely steeped when a soldier on horseback came riding along the beach. As soon as Brock saw the rider he began striding toward him.

"General Brock!" The solder dismounted and saluted. "I've been riding along the shoreline from Amherstburg, sir, in search of your fleet."

"Fleet is a rather grand word for it. What news?"

"Sir, the Americans have withdrawn from the British side of the Detroit River. They are back in their own fort."

Brock said nothing for a moment, just stared at the soldier disbelieving.

"They've *retreated*? Are you *sure*?"

"Yes sir. They crossed the river yesterday. They never attacked Fort Malden."

Brock turned away from us and walked down the beach alone. The officers stood about, watching him. He stopped, ran his hand through his hair, then swung about and walked briskly back.

"Prepare the boats. We must not rest again. We will row all day and all night, if need be."

The soldiers groaned in disbelief when they heard they were leaving, but they picked themselves up, brushed the sand from their wet clothes, and prepared the boats. Within an hour we were off.

The wind was good, and before long we had cleared Point Pelee. Brock pulled several maps out of his trunk and bent over them, ignoring everything else. The sun set, the sky darkened, but we rowed on.

I was the first to notice the black outline of the far shore dead ahead. It was my first sight of the United States. The enemy.

We sailed into a narrow channel. It was getting dark. In the distance a light shone from the top of a cliff.

"The fort," said Brock.

The men broke out the oars. We were so close now, and everyone was desperate to end this journey.

A line of torches began winding down a cliff. By the time we reached the wooden landing at the foot of the cliff we could make out their scarlet coats in the flickering light. The moment we docked Brock jumped out of the boat and exchanged hurried salutes with the officers at the landing. I recognized one of them—Procter. He was the one Brock had sent to take over command of the fort. I didn't recognize the man beside him, a short, rough-faced fellow—old, yet fierce-looking.

"General Brock." Procter saluted. "May I introduce Matthew Elliott, Superintendent of Indian Affairs at Amherstburg."

"Mr. Elliott," Brock nodded, "I am pleased by the reports of support among the Indians for our cause, and you are in no small measure the man we have to thank for it."

"Only my duty, sir." Elliott's voice was coarse but strong.

"Duty or not—" Brock stopped suddenly. A volley of musket fire crackled in the distance. "What is that?"

"The Indians, sir," replied Elliott. "They're celebrating your arrival."

"Make them stop," Brock snapped. "We have too little ammunition as it is."

Elliott scowled, but nodded and left the group.

Brock turned to Procter. "Are there dispatches for me?"

"Yes sir. Quite a number. From Fort George, and Niagara, and Governor-General Prevost in Montreal."

"I'll read them now. Fields, where are you?"

I stepped forward. "Here, sir."

"Find where I'm to be put and have my trunks sent there."

"Yes sir."

Then back to Procter. "I want you to call a meeting of all senior officers at this fort for midnight."

"Midnight, sir?"

"Midnight. We have no time to lose." He strode away from us toward the steep path that led to the fort. We followed.

"Gentlemen," he said quietly, as he climbed the path. "They had their opportunity, and they failed to pursue it. Now it is our turn. And we're not going to let it slip away.

"We're going to attack."

13

I found Brock's quarters inside the fort, and had the trunks and furniture sent there. The first thing I had to do was get his other uniform in shape. He'd been wearing the same one ever since we set sail, and it was time for a change. I unfolded the jacket, trousers and shirt, and cleaned and pressed them as best I could.

I had just about finished when a corporal pounded on the door.

"Private Fields!"

I ran to open it. "What is it?"

"General Brock says you know where his maps are. He wants them."

Of course I knew where his maps were—I'd already unpacked them and put them on his desk. I gathered them up and followed the corporal through the darkened yard of the fort to a small room. Brock was there, reading letters.

"Ah, here they are. Everything in order, Fields?"

"Yes sir. Have you eaten, sir?"

"Not yet. Maybe later. Is my other uniform ready?"

Before I could answer there was a knock, and Elliott entered, accompanied by an Indian.

I had seen Indians before, but none like this. He was tall—almost as tall as Brock—and dressed in a suit of deerskin, with fringes along the arms and legs. His moccasins were covered by porcupine quills. I'd heard that some sailors wore earrings. This man wore three rings—in his nose. A large silver medal hung from his neck on a necklace of coloured shells.

But his face was more striking than anything he wore. His bones seem sculpted, the smooth bronze skin covering high cheekbones, a broad chin, and a strong hooked nose. His eyes were dark and unreadable.

Elliott spoke. "General Brock, this is the Shawnee chief, Tecumseh."

Brock rose swiftly and held out his hand. "I am honoured to meet my fellow commander in our alliance against the Long Knives." (This is what the Indians called the Americans, because of the hunting knives they often carried.) Tecumseh gave Brock his hand.

. The two looked so different. Even among Englishmen Brock was unusually fair, with his pale skin and blond hair.

Tecumseh spoke. His voice was deep and rich. He spoke no English, and Elliott translated.

"I have received your request for my people not to fire their muskets. It is well advised. Muskets should be fired only at the enemy."

Brock nodded. "I am glad you agree. Your Indian force, I am told, numbers six hundred men."

Tecumseh nodded. "Some come each day, some leave each day. Like your militia."

Brock smiled ruefully. "Very much like our militia. But

we will need every man if we are to defeat the Americans."

"Are you going to attack?" Tecumseh asked directly.

"Yes. We must attack and soon."

Tecumseh nodded. "It is good to hear someone speak with a voice of action," Elliott translated. "When is your council of war?"

"In an hour."

Tecumseh nodded again. "I will be there." He turned to leave, then paused, and turned back to Brock. "It would be good for my people, if you would speak to them."

"I will speak to them in the morning."

"That is good." He spoke a few words to Elliott directly, then left. Elliott turned to go.

"Elliott," Brock stopped him. "What did he say to you at the end, that you didn't translate?"

Elliott's weathered face bent into a smile. "Sir, he said, 'This is a man.' "

Most of the next hour I spent locating the officers' mess and finding some bread and cold salted pork for Brock. By the time I returned the officers were already gathering for the meeting. Brock took the food without thinking and waved me away, then suddenly called out, "Fields."

"Sir!"

"Stay near the door. I may need you to run messages."

"Sir!"

He gave me a dark look. "And try to make a point of not hearing things."

I blushed. "Yes, *sir!*"

It was impossible though. Everything they said inside carried through the door. Especially when my ear was up against it.

Brock told the officers he was considering crossing the river and attacking Detroit. He asked each officer for his opinion. One by one they disagreed. The enemy outnumbered us. A superiority of two-to-one was needed to storm a fortified position. We could not count on the local militia. More American troops could be arriving at any time.

Only two people sided with Brock. One was an old militia officer who, I learned, had known Brock for years. The other was Tecumseh.

Brock listened, then began: "We must accept that we will always be outnumbered in this war—in men, in guns, in equipment. But the American general has shown us what he is made of. With superior forces, he failed to launch an assault on this fort—an assault that I am sure would have succeeded.

"I believe we can defeat their army. They fear us." He turned to Tecumseh. "They particularly fear you and your warriors.

"Here is what I propose: We will issue the militia with as many red coats as we have to spare, to make the Americans think our regular troops are more numerous. We will move the army to Sandwich, across the river from Detroit. At the same time, we will construct a gun battery and move what cannon we have into position there.

"Meanwhile, we will dispatch a courier to Michilimackinac in the north, with a letter. His real purpose is to be captured by the Americans. The letter will advise our forces there that we have five thousand Indians with us, ready to attack, and we need no more. Of course, we have not that number in our entire army, but this general may be frightened enough to believe it.

"I propose to cross the Detroit River in three days. The Indian forces will slip across the night before and hide themselves in the bush. If our landing is opposed, they will attack from the woods.

"My hope is that the Americans will choose to come out of the fort and attack us in the open. If they do, I believe our trained infantry will be superior to their untrained volunteers.

"That is my plan, gentlemen. I count on your support and loyalty in carrying it out."

There were no questions, no comments. Most of these officers had been opposed to Brock's plan since he first proposed it back in York. But there was no point in trying to change his mind.

The next morning after breakfast Brock walked out of the fort to talk to the Indians. He met them under an oak tree, just outside its walls. I watched from the gate, under a warm August sun and pale blue sky.

Hundreds of dark-skinned men with painted faces fanned out across the open field. I had never seen clothing so elaborate—rich bands of beads were draped over soft leathers decorated with more beads, feathers, and metal. Beside them the British in their scarlet uniforms looked plain and dull. Someone told me warriors from more than a dozen tribes were gathered on that field, from the Mohawk of Upper Canada to the Creek and Osage of the American South. They had been forged into an alliance by Tecumseh, and he alone held them together.

Brock spoke briefly, Elliott translating into several different tongues. The Americans were pushing the Indians farther and farther west, he told them. The British had always respected the Indians and their homelands. Now the Long Knives were threatening the homes of the British. If the children of the Great King were forced from these lands the Long Knives would take everything away, and leave the Indians with nothing.

"Together," he finished, "we shall protect both our peoples from the Long Knives. We will guarantee that your borders shall be respected, your people left free. We ask only that you help us as you have helped us before, in attacking this enemy we share."

The Indians looked upon him silently, glancing occasionally at each other, sometimes nodding, sometimes shaking their heads.

Then Tecumseh rose to speak. Standing there, beneath the oak, his long black hair flowing down his back, he seemed to me part general, part preacher.

He reminded them of past wars, of Indian villages destroyed by the American invaders, of women and children killed, of land seized by settlers and cleared of trees and wildlife.

"The soldiers of the Great King say they are our friends." He paused. "They are our friends when they need us. We do not forget that we have fought for the children of the Great King against the Long Knives before, and been

forgotten by the Great King when the fighting was over."
There was bitterness in his voice, and bitter nods of agreement met the words.

"But the British take little of our land, the Long Knives take much. The British ask only for skins and pelts. The Long Knives ask for everything.

"There is a British nation, and the nation of the Long Knives." His voice floated across the field of silent listeners. "We too must have a nation, to protect our lands and our people. The British have promised us this nation if we will fight for them. It is the only promise we have. Let us fight for our land!"

A great roar rose up from the Indians in the field. They raised their arms and shook them at the summer sky and screamed words I didn't know. Tecumseh quietly nodded to Brock. Brock nodded back.

My heart pounded in my chest. These were warriors! Wild, proud—they would fight for their land as fiercely as we would. More fiercely—this was more their land than ours.

Then came the betrayal.

I was laying out Brock's clothes that night when I heard him speaking in the hallway outside with Procter.

"I fear the Indians," worried Procter. "They are savage. In the heat of battle they can be unimaginably cruel."

"Yes," Brock replied. "But they are splendid fighters. And the Americans fear them. Their reputation alone is worth a regiment to me."

"Do you think their chief Tecumseh can control them?"

"Yes. He's a fine leader. He has united them in this dream of some kind of Indian nation. They believe him."

He was silent for a moment. Then, "Of course it will never happen. He could never keep them together. And I doubt we could permit it if he did."

He stepped into his room, but turned to Procter and didn't notice I was there.

"Let them go on believing, Procter. We need them now more than they need us."

"Good night, sir."

"Good night."

Then he saw me standing there, and saw the look on my face. Brock was lying to Tecumseh the way Uncle Will had lied to me. Deceit. That's all they knew. Deceit.

Brock's pale face pinkened. "What are you doing here?"

"Laying out your uniform."

"Well is it done?"

"Yes."

"Then leave."

I left quickly, avoiding his eyes. I stepped outside, paced across the parade ground, breathing heavily, walking to— where? There was nowhere to go. But I wanted to go. I wanted to get away from here.

I'd believed in him. He was the first man I'd ever really believed in. But he was no different. He lied when it suited him. Cheated when it served his needs. There was no one you could trust.

I wanted out of this army. I wanted to be away from this man.

The next day was one endless rushing about. There were a thousand things to be done—reorganizing the local militia, putting the cannons in place across the river from the American fort, marching the troops up to Sandwich, making the boats ready for the crossing.

Brock was in constant motion, inspecting troops, inspecting equipment, giving orders and more orders.

I kept out of his way. There wasn't much for me to do, except look after his laundry and his horse. (A difficult, high-strung horse—Alfred had been left at Niagara.) The general ate most of his meals in the officers' mess, and he seldom called for me. When we did see each other, neither said much.

I couldn't be sure if he knew what I'd heard. If he did, he probably didn't care. Why would he care? What would it matter to him, that his batman knew he was going to betray the Indians?

Why should it matter to me? Mama always told me the only two things in this world you could really trust were the love of God and your own two hands. What did it matter to me what these British soldiers were up to? Better to do your job and keep your ears shut.

But I couldn't. I felt sick. When I left the farm it seemed to me everyone good was dead and everyone alive was bad. Brock had changed that. I had admired him, grown to trust him, and he seemed to trust me.

Now I knew he couldn't be trusted, either. There was no one on earth you could trust. And I had my doubts about the love of God.

Brock sent over a boat with three officers, demanding the surrender of Fort Detroit. It was ridiculous—they outnumbered us and outgunned us. The answer came back that if we wanted their fort, we'd have to fight for it. It sounded as though their General Hull wasn't quite so frightened after all.

As soon as the reply came back we let them have it with our cannon at Sandwich. The American cannon answered, but the river was half a mile wide, and many of the shells from both sides damaged nothing but the grass.

It didn't matter—Brock was out to scare the Americans, not blow them up.

That night we slept under a sky littered with stars. At least we would have slept, except for the dull thunder of the cannon fire that punctured the night air and filled it with bitter smoke.

But then, who could sleep anyway? We were going into battle tomorrow.

The Indians had already left. They slipped into their canoes as soon as it was dark and glided across the still river. I had seen Brock with Elliott and Tecumseh talking together by the river's edge, just before the Indian chief left to join his men. They seemed to be talking over a plan. What the plan was, nobody knew.

The dawn was beautiful. As we gathered along the shore, a mist rose off the river, softening the light and blending the colours of the grass and water and trees. Brock was in the first wave of boats. I was in the second, on a flat scow, holding the reins of the unhappy horse.

As long as I live I will never forget the sight of our army crossing the river. The water was a smooth sheet. The boats glided silently across, each filled with men in brilliant scarlet uniforms. Just downstream, two warships sat at anchor, guarding our crossing. I knew I should be afraid. I was going into my first battle. But instead I was filled with a pride that choked my throat at this beautiful army crossing into America.

We landed about three miles downstream from Detroit. As soon as the boats touched the shore the men were hurried off and hustled into formation by shouting, sweating sergeants. The Indians came out of the bush to watch us. They were there to attack any Americans who tried to stop the landing, but the Americans were still inside the fort. I threaded my way through the pushing, rushing soldiers, the horse in tow, until I found Brock.

He was in the middle of a knot of officers, looking at a map and pointing in the direction of the fort. Elliott was with him. He knew this country as well as anyone born here.

"... If you say so, Elliott, we'll form the line here," Brock said, pointing to the map, "and wait for them to come out."

An Indian on horseback galloped toward us. Brock

looked up quickly. "What is it?"

The Indian spoke to Elliott, who turned to Brock. "There are American troops about three miles away, marching toward the fort. Maybe four hundred of them."

"Damn!" It was the first time I'd heard Brock swear. But in a moment he'd put his mask of reserve back on.

"Well, this changes things. Troops to our rear, a fort in front. We are pinned."

"Sir, shouldn't we withdraw?" Procter's face was pale, and he seemed to be swallowing a lot.

"I think not." Brock frowned at the map. "To withdraw would be equal to defeat. Well," he rolled up the map. "We shall have to attack the fort before their reinforcements arrive."

"But sir—!"

"Form your troops into a single column," Brock ordered. "Put extra distance between the units. They may forget to count and think we have more men than we do."

"Sir," Procter protested. "If we attack the fort we'll be torn apart by their cannon."

"I think not." Brock shook his head. "We'll follow the river bank. Our cannon at Sandwich will protect us until we're almost at the town. See here on the map—there's an orchard just before the town, and in front of it a ravine running parallel to the town walls. The ravine will protect us from their guns. From the ravine we will attack the town, and from the town attack the fort.

"Gentlemen, I have decided. We march in fifteen minutes. Where's my horse?"

"Here, sir." I stepped forward.

"Fields, return to Sandwich. I don't want to lose another batman."

"But sir—"

"That's enough." He mounted the horse and rode off.

I wandered slowly back to the boats, ignoring the soldiers that pushed past me. It wasn't right. I had come this far. I wanted to fight. It didn't matter why we were fighting—these men were going to fight, and I was in a uniform, and it was my duty to fight.

Confusion tore at me. The night before I'd wanted to leave Brock, leave this army. But now I was here. I didn't want to turn my back on it.

I was standing by the water's edge, leaning against the side of a boat, when I saw Stanton. He was marching along the shoreline with the forty men of his company behind him. I recognized the men—it was good to see Maitland again. It was even good to see MacPherson.

I left the boats and ran toward them. Stanton gave me a swift look.

"Fields, what are you doing here?"

"Looking for a company to join, sir. General Brock doesn't need me right now."

He frowned. "Looking to join the fight, are you? You may wish you'd stayed behind, before this is through."

"I want to fight, sir. I have my musket."

He shrugged. "I can't keep track of who is in my company at a time like this. Anyone could attach himself to the rear."

I grinned, and saluted, and ran to the back of the column. I had a bit of trouble falling into step. It had been a while since I'd marched with troops.

We followed the bank of the river. The British war ships sailed along beside us. Across the river our cannon continued to pound away at the fort. From the front of the column the sound of fifes and drums drifted through the air—a tune they called "British Grenadiers." The music filled your heart, made you want to fight.

Before long we came into sight of the wooden palisade, about twice as high as a man, surrounding the town of Detroit. Beyond that stood the stone walls of the fort.

"Look at that." The private beside me jerked his head.

"Look at what?"

"The gates of the town."

I strained to see. In the middle of the palisade was a gate. And something . . . there! Two cannons perched on top of the palisade, pointed right at us, one on either side of the gate, the gun crews standing ready. Suddenly I was sweating. They'd be using grapeshot—dozens of musket balls inside a canvas bag. When the bag split open the balls went everywhere. One shot could cut down a company like a scythe going through hay.

My mouth went dry. I was shaking. I couldn't take my eyes off those guns. We were close enough now to see the blue uniforms of the Yankee soldiers manning the cannon, lit fuses in their hands. Why didn't they fire? The music of the fife and drums sounded hideous now, like some mad song played by a lunatic. We were going to die and they were playing music. Why didn't they fire? I'd never get to use my musket, never even see the enemy. I'd simply fall here, my chest ripped open by a musket ball.

And for what? What was I dying for?

Brock was at the front of the column. The gold braids on his shoulders glinted in the morning sun. He'd be the first to die. An officer rode up to him, pointed to the rear of the column, seemed to be urging Brock back, but the general shook his head and the officer gave up. Brock would be the first to go down. The rest of us would be next.

Why didn't they fire?

"Column . . . by companies . . . left *wheel!*"

Suddenly we were marching into the orchard. There were trees between us and the guns. Some protection, not much.

And then I saw the ravine—deep and wide, with steep slopes. There was a stone farmhouse at the bottom, and Brock was already riding toward it. We tumbled down the slope. We were safe.

The men around me began taking deep breaths. A few exchanged weak grins. We'd all been watching those guns.

It only took a few minutes before everyone was in the ravine. Now we had time to take a good look at what faced us. The wooden palisade was maybe fourteen feet high. You could see the shingled roofs of houses poking above it. About two hundred yards beyond, the stone walls of the fort rose up from the top of a hill. How would we ever get up those walls? What was Brock *thinking?*

I heard them before I saw them. When I saw them my heart stopped. Indians, hundreds of Indians, burst out of the dense bush on our left, dancing and shouting and screaming for blood. Their faces and chests were bare, streaked with purple and red dye. They waved cruel-looking tomahawks above their heads. The warriors danced in a long line, then disappeared into the bush. But the line never seemed to end. Always there were more—hundreds more, maybe thousands—thrusting themselves into the clearing, screaming bloody vengeance against the Long Knives, then disappearing into the dark woods.

Where had they come from? There couldn't have been more than six hundred Indians at Amherstburg, and here there were thousands. They were a great army all by themselves.

Then I saw it. One warrior's face was painted in bright purple, with gold streaks. He'd been among the first Indians to come out of the bush. And here he was again, dancing and whooping in the long line. How could he ... it was a hoax! The Indians were doubling back in the bush and joining the line again. They were the same Indians, over and over, appearing and disappearing. And giving the impression of thousands.

The soldiers rested on their muskets and watched the Indian display, partly in awe, partly in fear. Then I saw a militia private throw back his head and laugh. He'd figured it out.

Suddenly someone showed up with bottles of brandy and wine and loaves of bread. The farmer who owned the stone house was descended from British stock, and happy to have redcoats on his land. He was offering breakfast. I grabbed a piece of bread. Amazingly, I was hungry.

"The gates are opening!"

We grabbed our muskets and scrambled into line of battle. Had the Americans decided to come out and fight?

Unless they did, we'd have to attack the town. And no one was looking forward to that.

We waited for the line of Yankee blue to march out into the field. But all that emerged were two American officers walking stiffly toward us, carrying a white flag. A white flag! We couldn't believe it.

The Yankees' faces were clenched in anger. When they reached the ravine, they stopped and saluted.

"We seek permission to speak with your commanding officer."

Stanton stepped out of the ravine and saluted them. "Follow me."

He led them to the farmhouse. The Indians stopped their war dance, and stared silently. We were all wondering—what was going on? Were they surrendering? Why would they surrender? Maybe our cannon had killed their general. Maybe their troops were deserting. Maybe they'd been fooled by the Indians. The Indians had almost fooled me, and I was on their side.

Or maybe it was a trap. Maybe the Yankees were about to attack.

The American officers left the farmhouse and marched back to the town. Stanton returned and told us to be ready.

"What did they say, captain?" "Tell us, captain," the men begged.

Stanton raised his hand. "The Americans have asked for a three-day truce. General Brock has given them three hours. Then we attack. Check your muskets."

But it was only minutes before the Americans returned. This time two British officers stepped out of the ravine to meet them. We watched them speak together in the field, the blue and the red, their hands resting on their swords, just in case.

Suddenly one of the Yankees pulled his sword from its sheath. For a moment we tensed. Was this the end of the truce? But he just handed the sword to the British officer, who took it and saluted the American.

The man beside me, a wiry old veteran who needed a shave, let out a whoop an Indian would be proud of.

"What does it mean?" I grabbed his arm. All around me men were cheering, throwing their hats in the air. "What does it mean?"

"What do you think it means?" The soldier grinned at me.

"They've surrendered, lad! They've surrendered!"

15

Once again we were marching in column, and once again the flutes played "British Grenadiers," but now we weren't staring at guns. We were marching into Detroit. And Detroit was ours.

We passed through the palisade into the town. The worried, curious faces of women and children peered from the windows and doors of the houses. As soon as I entered I saw two buildings with large holes in their walls. Our cannon fire had done more damage than I'd thought.

Hundreds of Yankee soldiers lined the side of the road. They were throwing their muskets and swords onto great piles. Many of them were crying. Some shook their fists at us and cursed—others cursed their leaders.

I noticed a young officer. He was standing a few feet in from the road. Tears streamed down his face. As I watched he pulled his sword out of its sheath. Crying, he broke the sword over his knee and threw the two pieces into the mud.

Most of the Americans just stared at us, their faces blank. They must have been wondering where the great army was that had forced their surrender. Surely they hadn't given over everything to these few soldiers?

But they had. Their general had been deceived. He'd been deceived by the militiamen wearing the red coats of the British infantry. He'd been deceived by our cannon into thinking we could batter his fort to dust.

Mostly he'd been deceived by a few hundred Indians, who looked like a great army and broke his heart with fear.

Fort Detroit had surrendered, which meant the British now controlled everything from Fort Michilimackinac in the north to the Ohio River in the south, a land as big as Upper Canada itself. Our army, short on guns, short on ammunition, short on everything, now had thousands of extra guns and dozens of cannon, captured from the Yankees, to be used against the Yankees. What's more, word was already spreading of a fortune in American gold to be distributed among the men. Rumour had it we were all about to get six months' pay, and not one of us had fired a shot.

A soldier ran past us, holding a flag. A few minutes later we saw him on the roof of a building inside the fort, hauling down the Yankee Stars and Stripes. Up went the Union Jack in its place. We cheered. The Yankees turned their faces away.

We passed through the gate into Fort Detroit. The walls were at least twelve feet thick. How would we have got inside? It didn't matter—we walked inside.

A dozen British soldiers came out of a large building in the middle of the fort. They were escorting an American prisoner.

"It's Hull!" someone called out. "It's General Hull!"

I craned my neck to look. He was old and heavy, with

grey hair and a grey beard. As he got closer I saw his face clearly. His eyes were half closed, his head was bowed. His skin was a sick, yellow colour, covered in a sheen of sweat. He was chewing something furiously—tobacco. The juice was dribbling out the side of his mouth, staining his beard and uniform. He looked pathetic.

"Eyes *front!*" Stanton snapped angrily. We looked away. As they led him out of the fort we could hear cries of "Traitor!" "Coward!" The Yankee troops cursed their general to his face.

We formed into companies on the parade ground. A detachment of American soldiers formed across from us. One of them stepped forward carrying a folded banner— the regimental colours of the defending troops. This officer was nothing like Hull. His face burned with anger, pride, and shame. He saluted stiffly, and handed the banner to Colonel Procter, who saluted in return, took the banner, and gave it to one of our men.

The surrender was complete.

Brock and Tecumseh entered the fort together, side by side on horseback. The twin generals had come to survey their conquest. Brock owed this victory to Tecumseh. The Yankees' fear of those Indian tomahawks had done more than any cannon could do.

As I watched the Shawnee chief, proud but grave at Brock's side, the joy of victory faded out of me. Tecumseh had given Brock Detroit. He had kept his word. Did he know Brock's word meant nothing?

That night, back on our own side of the river, we stood around bonfires outside the fort and sang and arm-wrestled and drank rum. The officers made a point of looking the other way.

I walked about alone, beyond the edge of revellers, holding a bottle of rum someone had handed me. I hadn't been allowed to drink rum with the other men before, but now I was a veteran, and no one seemed to care. I took a long drink, and another. It burned my throat and made my gut churn, but my head felt light and free.

Brock hadn't sent for me. He seemed to have forgotten all about me. I wanted to forget about him. The battle was over. The local militia would be returning to their farms soon. Maybe I should go with them.

I wanted out. The others could sing and tell lies about their bravery when no one fired a shot. I knew the truth. The Indians were celebrating around their own campfires, a few hundred yards away. Their shouts echoed across the night air. They had reason to celebrate—they'd taken Fort Detroit for us.

But really they had no reason to celebrate at all. If every one of them had died for their nation, they'd still be no closer to getting it.

"Hey, look!"

I turned toward the shout. Half a dozen Shawnee warriors were standing at the edge of one of our campfires. The singing stopped. The men stood up quickly. They weren't any less afraid of Indians than the Yankees were.

One of the warriors stepped forward silently. He offered a sergeant a belt made of beads and shells braided together. It was called a wampum, and the Indians valued them highly.

The sergeant hesitated. "Take it, sergeant," someone whispered. "Quick, before they change their minds."

The sergeant reached forward and took the wampum. "Well now, thank you," he nodded. "Thank you."

"Give them some rum."

"Yeah, give it to them."

The sergeant handed a bottle to the warrior. "Here. Drink it in good health."

The Indian shook his head. One warrior spoke urgently, but he was cut off sharply by the others.

"Well, now." The sergeant looked to his men and then back. "If you won't drink, you can at least share the fire."

He motioned them toward the blaze. The warriors stepped forward slowly, looking nervously at each other.

"Play something, Tom. Go on."

An accordion wheezed out a jig. The Indians smiled. One of them did a little dance. Everyone laughed.

Blood pounded angrily in my head. These soldiers were singing and dancing with the Indians. Part of me said that this was good, that this was how understanding started.

But the rum drowned that out. All I could see were these men acting like old comrades toward the Indians while our leaders were betraying them. It was all fake. It was all unreal.

I stepped toward the fire. "This is wrong." No one heard me. I shouted it. "This is *wrong!*"

The music stopped. Faces turned to me, glowing in the light of the fire.

I moved toward the warrior who had made the gift of the wampum. "Don't you know they're lying to you? They're not your friends. They just want you to do their fighting for them. They want you to fight the Long Knives, so they can win their war and then take your land."

"For the love of God, private—"

But I wouldn't stop. "You think you're fighting for your homes? We're not going to let you keep your homes. We're lying to you!"

"Are you crazy—"

"We're lying to you! We're going to take your land, just like the Long Knives. We may not fight you for it, but we'll take it just the same. We just need you right now . . . we just—"

"He's going to start a fight."

"Someone stop him!"

The warriors gazed at me steadily. They couldn't know what I was saying, but they could see my expression. Did they understand? How could I make them understand?

"We just need you to fight for us." I was crying. "We *need* you to fight for us, so we don't have to fight ourselves, that's all. You should go. You should leave us. Go back to your lands. We're not worth dying for—"

"Fields!"

A hand grabbed my arm. I swung around in fury. "Just try to—"

"Atten . . . *shun!*"

An officer's uniform, a command. My mind raged against it, but a deeper instinct obeyed. I snapped to attention.

It was Stanton, his face cold with fury. "What's going on here?"

"He tried to pick a fight with the Indians, sir."

"No! I—"

"Be quiet!" Stanton turned to the men at the campfire. "Perhaps it would be best if the Indians returned to their own people." He bowed to them and gestured toward the Indian fires. The warrior who had given the wampum nodded gravely and spoke to his men. They disappeared into the dark.

"The rest of you have had enough celebration for one night. Turn in. Fields, come with me."

"Sir—"

"Come with ME!"

We walked in silence toward the fort. We were almost at its gates when he wheeled around. "I cannot believe this. We have just won a victory. Our general is a hero. And when he can't find his cuff links for the victory dinner, he discovers his batman has disappeared. And I'm sent to find him, because I recommended him in the first place. And when I do find him, he's about to start an Indian war!"

"I wasn't—"

"Do you know what could have happened? Do you know how much we need the Indians? What if a fight had started? What if it had got out of control? You could have undone everything that was accomplished here today."

I couldn't speak. That wasn't what I'd meant. A pain stabbed at my head. I felt dizzy.

"I'm confining you to the blockhouse, Fields. General Brock will decide what to do with you." He shook his head.

"I was a fool to place any trust in you."

He marched me to the blockhouse and handed me over to the guard. I was placed in a tiny room, with a straw pallet. I curled up on the pallet and shut my eyes against my pounding head.

He was wrong. I hadn't meant to start a fight. What had I meant?

What had I done?

16

I leaned over the bow of the *Chippawa*, trying not to be sick. Sailing in a large schooner in the middle of a storm was something new for me, and my insides didn't like it. The waves heaved us up to the sky, then threw us into great ravines of grey-green water. I wanted to leave my body.

The sea-sickness was a relief, in a way. It took my mind off my own thoughts. I had wanted out of this army. Well, I might be getting out, but not the way I'd hoped. The least I was going to get was a whipping, the worst—jail and a dishonourable discharge. Brock had ordered me onto the *Chippawa* before he boarded it. He was going to deal with me personally. I tried not to think about what sort of dealing he had in mind.

We were on our way east to Fort Erie. Brock was rushing to Niagara to see what the Americans were up to. The first victory was so easy that most soldiers were eager to take on the Yankees again. But all I had to look forward to was punishment and disgrace.

"Sail ho!" I lifted my head. Another schooner was approaching us from the east. The thought half-formed in my mind that it was an American warship, that we were going to be attacked and sunk in the middle of the lake. My stomach looked forward to it.

But then I noticed the British ensign snapping in the wind, and I remembered that the Great Lakes belonged to us; the Americans had no ships to fight us with.

The two schooners drew alongside. Brock came out of his cabin in the *Chippawa's* stern and watched as the other ship launched a boat carrying a British officer. He clambered up the net we'd thrown over the side and snapped to attention in front of his general.

"General Brock, sir, Governor-General Prevost sends his compliments from Quebec, sir. I am to give you this message: Great Britain and the United States of America have ceased hostilities. An armistice has been signed, while both sides negotiate an end to the war."

Brock's mouth dropped open, then quickly shut. "An *armistice*? When?"

"It was signed August sixteenth, sir. The day Detroit surrendered. Of course, both sides were unaware of your victory there at the time. Still, the truce holds."

"Come." Brock turned on his heel and stalked back into his cabin, the officer following.

The soldiers and sailors gossiped. What did the armistice mean? Was the war over? Had we won?

Everyone waited for news. I waited, too. But I was more worried about my own future than the future of the war.

I was asleep below decks (the storm had ended and my seasickness was ebbing, bit by bit) when the guard shook me awake.

"Come on," he ordered. "The general wants to see you."

He led me to the back of the ship and knocked on a door. I recognized the voice. "Yes."

I stepped into a tiny room, barely big enough for a desk and a bed. We both had to stoop a bit to keep from hitting our heads on the ceiling.

Brock was tearing through his large trunk, throwing clothes and papers in every direction. "The brandy, Fields. Where's the brandy? You always keep it in this trunk. One night, *one night*, I choose a glass of brandy before bed, and it's not here!

"It's in the small trunk, sir." The small trunk was beside me. I opened the lid and pulled out the bottle.

He glared at me. "Why did you put it there? You've always kept it in the big trunk."

"No sir. I always keep it in the small trunk."

"Don't contradict me, boy!"

"Yes sir."

He grabbed the brandy and poured himself a large glass. "You've gotten yourself into quite a mess, Fields. Stanton told me you tried to start a fight with an Indian."

"I did not, sir."

The denial seemed to surprise him. "You contradict Captain Stanton?"

"No sir. Captain Stanton didn't know what was happening when he arrived. He misunderstood."

"He says you were drunk."

"I think I was, sir."

"You've become quite useless, Fields." The tone was

petulant, impatient, like some offended school teacher. "You're sullen, unreliable. I can't depend on you any more. And now this. I should have you whipped. Or worse."

"Yes sir."

"Certainly I can't have you as my batman. You will be reassigned to your regiment as soon as we reach shore."

"Yes sir. May I be discharged from the army, sir?"

It surprised him. He put down his brandy. "Is that what you want?"

"Yes sir."

He looked at me for a moment, almost sadly, and then his face hardened. "Very well. If you want to go, go. We have no room for cowards."

The blood rushed to my face. "I am not a coward!"

He stepped toward me angrily. "You are insubordinate and untrustworthy and mutinous and probably a coward, and I cannot believe I am even speaking to you, when I should simply have you flogged."

"Flog me if you want," I shouted, hoarse with anger, "but I'm no coward!"

For a moment I thought he was going to call the sentry. He looked at the door, half-opened his mouth, then closed it and turned away.

"I have never endured such insolence from a soldier." He picked up his brandy. "But then you're not a regular soldier, are you? You're a colonial. One of the people I have been sent here to protect. Why, I don't know."

He walked over to the tiny window. "In England you would know your place." He stared out at the black sky. "You would never raise your voice against a gentleman.

People know their place in England.

"But not here. There is too much of the American in you all. You're rude to your betters, say whatever you think, have no respect. You're not worth fighting for." He paused. "You're certainly not worth dying for."

"At least I've never lied." The words came from . . . somewhere. I knew I shouldn't have said it. I was in worse trouble now than for anything I'd done at Detroit. But worse than the punishment, worse than anything he could do to me, was knowing that he'd lied. If only he hadn't lied. . . .

Brock turned from the window. A pink blush coloured his pale skin. He gripped the brandy in his hand. "Are you suggesting that I have lied?"

The truth. Speak the truth. "You know I heard you and Colonel Procter. You're going to betray the Indians."

Now you've done it.

"You've committed treason." He seemed more surprised than angry. "What you've said is treasonous."

"Treason to you. To me it's just the truth."

I waited. Things had gone too far. A moment ago I was out of the army, free. Now I was a word away from being shot. But at least it was out.

Brock watched the brandy as he swirled it around in the glass. I was surprised to see the tired smile that suddenly crossed his face. "You're right of course. We probably have betrayed the Indians. They believe they will win their land from this war, and they won't. And I know they won't, but I let Tecumseh believe it."

He drained the brandy in the glass, then poured himself another and sat down. "If it were up to me I would let them keep their land. Many of us feel an Indian buffer state between British North America and the United States would be good protection. But it won't happen. Too many settlers are arriving. They need farms. The Indians have the land the settlers need. Sooner or later we will take the Indians' land from them. This is not what I wish for, Fields. It is only what I know will happen."

He raised his glass to his lips, then lowered it without drinking. "I find it . . . extraordinary, to be telling you this." He shook his head a little.

I didn't say anything. I didn't know what to say. He wasn't really talking to me, anyway. He was talking to himself, or to the brandy.

"But then you deserve to know," he continued. "You do seem to me the best and worst of these settlers. Obstinate, uncivilized, rude. But honest, also, and proud. I am sorry I called you a coward."

I felt guilty, somehow. "I didn't mean to call you a liar, sir."

"Well, but you did." He straightened up in his chair. "And I am. I needed the Indians at Detroit. I will need them again at Niagara. This armistice is a trick by the Americans to give them time to bring men and supplies to the front. We were fools to accept it, and we'll pay."

He got up from his chair. "So I will lie to your Indians again. I need them if I am to have another victory. I am a general, Fields. Victory is what is expected of me. For victory, I would lie to God himself."

I stood there, uncertain, not knowing what to do, even what to feel.

He began to arrange papers on his desk. "I will see to your discharge when we reach Fort Erie. You will not be charged with treason—unless, of course, you repeat anything that has been said here."

"Sir—I would like to continue, sir, as your batman." Why? I don't know why. Except I didn't see him now as a liar. No, it was more complicated than that.

He looked at me for a long moment. "Are you sure?"

I nodded. "Yes, sir. Very sure. I . . . I'm sorry, sir."

He returned to his papers. "Very well, Fields. That will be all."

I turned sharply on my heel and left the cabin. But I didn't return below. I walked along the deck of the ship, watched the black waves with their shining white crests roll against the hull, stared up at the great bowl of stars shining through the rigging that creaked in the fresh west wind.

And wondered when I would begin to understand the world.

17

"Why don't they attack? The armistice ended weeks ago, and still they sit there. Why in God's name don't they attack?"

His name was Major Thomas Evans. Brock liked him. He was brave and confident—like his general. And he asked questions other officers were afraid to ask.

The two of them stood on the sloping ground in front of Fort George—Evans and Brock, watching the American fires on the shore only a few hundred yards away. A fierce fall wind whipped at their cloaks. They braced their feet to keep from being pushed toward the river below. I stood well back, holding Alfred's reins.

Brock shook his head. "I don't understand. If I were them, I would attack. I would have attacked long ago."

There were four of them for every one of us. An American army of eight thousand men stretched along the Niagara river, with guns and ammunition and a thirst to avenge Detroit. We had barely two thousand, defending a front thirty-six miles long, from Fort Erie in the south to Fort George in the north.

The Americans might attack from several points, say at Fort Erie and Fort George. If they did that they could break through our lines and come at us from the rear. To prevent it, Brock had to split his forces, putting most of his strength at either end. But that left us weak in the middle. If they attacked in force there, they could cut us in half.

And we were losing control of the lakes. We knew they were building ships for Lake Erie and Lake Ontario. And just a few days ago Yankee troops in small boats had crept up on two of our ships anchored off Fort Erie and boarded them. They captured one and destroyed the other. When Brock heard he pounded his desk. "They will command the lakes. If they command the lakes, the war is over."

No matter how you looked at it, they had the advantage. But it was already the middle of October, and they did nothing. They just sat there and waited. We didn't know why, though we heard stories. Almost every day Yankee deserters tried swimming across the river. The currents and whirlpools claimed a lot of them. Those that survived told of troops sleeping without tents and walking barefoot, of officers fighting among themselves and refusing to obey orders.

The Yankees had started this war, but their politicians and generals didn't seem eager to spend time or money fighting it.

Still, things weren't that much better here. It was a bitter fall. The rain soaked everything—we lived in mud. There were fights among the men, even talk of mutiny. Many of our militia had gone back to their farms. Brock let them go.

I had never seen Brock more worried. He was an impatient general, and hated waiting. But he had no choice except to wait. We could never attack the Americans with our small force. Anyway, Governor-General Prevost had told Brock not to attack—he was still afraid of "provoking" the Americans.

It was hard for Brock. On the one hand, everyone called him the saviour of Canada. When we got to Fort Erie six weeks ago he had rushed to Kingston to consult with Prevost and inspect the troops. No one could praise him enough. He was the most popular man in British North America, a brilliant general, a heroic leader.

But did it matter? The Americans were stronger than they'd ever been. Brock had moved every uniform he could find to Niagara, strengthened the fortifications. When two hundred Mohawk and other tribes of the Six Nations arrived and offered to help fight the Long Knives, Brock embraced their leaders. But the Yankees still outnumbered us four to one.

Why didn't they attack?

Brock and Evans turned away from the river. "Take Alfred back to the fort," Brock told me. "I shall walk awhile."

I snapped a salute and pulled on Alfred's reins. I saluted Brock a lot now. It was the way things were—formal, correct. We both liked it that way. Once I had almost worshipped Brock. Then I had almost hated him. Now . . . what should I feel? I'd called him a liar, but he wasn't a liar. Not really. He was doing what he had to do, doing what was expected of him.

But still . . . the Indians were fighting for him, would die for him, and they would never get what he promised them.

What was right? How should I feel? I think maybe I felt a bit frightened of him. And I think he was a little frightened of me.

That's strange to say. Brock, the hero of Upper Canada, commander of all its troops, frightened of a fifteen-year-old batman?

But I don't think anyone had seen him the way I'd seen him in the cabin that night. He rarely showed what he was thinking, let alone how he felt. Maybe what he said that night frightened him. Maybe, because he said it to me, he was a little frightened of me.

So we both retreated into our roles. I tried to become the perfect batman—always available, but silent, like some helpful ghost. He acted like the perfect officer. It suited both of us.

I served Brock dinner in his quarters that night. He almost always ate alone now, munching on his boiled pork or beef with his head bent over a map. At York he had talked out loud to his maps, argued with them, I think dreamed victories with them. Now he stared at them silently, studying the same hills over and over, maybe waiting for a clue, a sign, a way out. He was so different now. Before, everything was action. Now, everything was waiting. And the maps seemed to hold no clues.

I was just taking away his tray when booted footsteps clicked down the hall. We both looked up—everyone knew the step of an officer in a hurry.

Evans appeared. Whatever the news, it was bad. His face was drawn, tight. I left the room quickly, not waiting to be told, and stood guard at the door, to give them privacy and to overhear.

"Mutiny, sir. At Queenston. One company of regulars is in revolt, threatening to shoot the officers. Captain Dennis has written asking for help."

It wasn't surprising. The strain of waiting for the battle was telling on everyone. The men were wet and unhappy and worried about dying. Brock would take it badly, though. It was one thing for the militia to ask to go home. But when British troops were disloyal . . . .

He didn't say anything for a moment. I heard him pace about. He would be composing himself, forcing his temper down, running his hand through his hair, trying to push his mind to deal with the situation.

"I want you to go there in the morning," he said finally. "Bring the ringleaders here. We will have to make an example of them."

"Yes sir."

There was weariness in Evans's voice. He knew what he was about to do. A few years ago some troops had mutinied at Fort George. Brock had the leaders executed in front of the men. The story went that he cried as he watched them being shot. But they were still shot.

"There's something else you can do when you're there," Brock continued, ignoring Evans's reluctance. "Cross over to the American side under a flag of truce. Tell them I will exchange prisoners."

"Yes sir."

"And Evans—you might take note of whatever you happen to see."

"I'll report immediately, sir."

"But most important, we must crush this mutiny quickly and severely."

"Yes, sir."

Evans's step was slower and heavier when he left.

The next day I tried to be even less noticeable than usual around Brock. He was in a black mood, snapping at the officers and men and, when he noticed me, snapping at me. Our one advantage over the Yankees was our trained and disciplined infantry. And now the infantry was mutinying.

I groaned to myself when a messenger came and said Brock needed me. He was eating with the officers that night. His uniform was already laid out for tomorrow—I'd hoped to keep out of his way until Evans was back and the mutiny settled. But it was too much to hope for.

I reached the door of the officers' mess just as a young private came out, sweating. He gave me a quick look that said it was hell in there, then scurried off. I took a breath, and knocked on the door.

"Come."

Half a dozen officers were sitting around the large oak table, their food cold and half eaten. Brock was at the far end of the table.

"Private Fields." He was even more stern and formal than usual. "We would like to ask you some questions. You may rest assured your answers will be treated in confidence, and nothing you say will be used against you. Do you understand?"

"Yes sir." I didn't understand.

"You were born in Upper Canada and volunteered for the service just before the outbreak of war, is that correct?" I nodded. He knew that.

"Have you heard about the mutiny at Queenston?"

I swallowed. Was I in trouble? Should I lie? But I knew Brock better than to lie to him.

"Yes sir."

"It has, I take it, become common knowledge among the men."

I panicked. He knew I'd overheard his conversation with Evans. He thought I'd told everyone. But I hadn't. I hadn't said a word. The soldiers got wind of the revolt the way soldiers get wind of everything that happens.

"I didn't say a word, sir!"

Brock almost smiled. "I'm sure you didn't, Fields. You have always impressed me with your ability to hear things you shouldn't and not repeat them."

The other officers chuckled. They all had batmen, and probably all shared the same jokes about them.

"There are other colonial regulars in this army. Do you think they are loyal?"

It shocked me. A British officer was asking a volunteer private if the other volunteers were loyal. Now I knew why the private had been sweating. He was one of the regulars from England. He'd probably been asked the same question about them.

"All the men are loyal, sir." It was the smart thing to say, and true, too. I'd never heard anyone talk mutiny. They complained a lot—the food tasted better if you complained about it. But they were loyal.

"I'm glad to hear it, Fields." Brock leaned back in his chair. "I have always believed the men were loyal. But as you know, I was not entirely correct."

"Every man I know is loyal, sir. We would follow you anywhere." We already had.

Brock nodded. "I sent for you, Fields, because I know you are not afraid to speak the truth—" he grimaced, "no matter how unpleasant. I am reassured by your report. That is all."

I turned to go. I was sweating, too. Being honest around British officers had its price.

I was halfway to the door when Evans burst in. He was soaking wet. His breath came in gasps. He didn't bother to salute, but threw himself into a chair.

"General Brock, the Americans . . ." He was so out of breath he could barely speak. " . . . The Americans are about to attack."

"Get him some wine." Brock was out of his chair and striding toward Evans. I ran to the sideboard, poured a glass of port, and brought it to Evans. He drank the glass in a gulp.

"Thank you. Another please. I haven't eaten yet today."

I gathered up some bread and cheese from the table, and brought over the decanter of port.

"What happened, Evans?" Brock grabbed Evans's chair and leaned over him. For a moment I thought he was going to grab the major, shake the news loose.

"Sir—" Evans gulped some more port, and bit off a slice of the bread. Now his mouth was too full to talk. I thought Brock was going to break something.

"Sir." Evans finally found his voice. "I arrived at Queenston to find it under a hail of musket fire from across the river. Captain Dennis said the Americans had made a habit of this, lately. I decided I must see at once what was happening. I set off across the river with the local militia captain." He offered a wry smile. "The snipers were most unsporting. I believe they used our flag of truce as a target.

"When I reached the far shore, I was greeted by one of their majors. No senior officer would speak with me. They said sir—" he straightened up in his chair. "They said they could not discuss an exchange of prisoners *for another two days*. Sir, I am convinced they plan to attack tomorrow."

"Nonsense." One of the colonels lit a cigar. "That means nothing. Their senior officers weren't available. A junior officer simply wanted to avoid taking responsibility."

"That is most likely what happened." Brock let go of Evans's chair. He looked disappointed. For a moment he had hoped the battle was finally about to begin. But Evans had simply got carried away.

"Sir, there's more." Evans rose unsteadily from his chair. "There were thousands of troops on the American side. Regular infantry, and savage-looking militia. I'm certain they have massed much of their army across the river from Queenston Heights."

"That makes no sense," another officer protested. "Queenston is in the centre of our line of defence. Why would they attack there, when a flanking attack would be more certain of success?"

Brock was standing absolutely still, staring at the regimental colours draped on one wall. Everyone knew that stance—he was trying to reach out across the miles and enter the mind of an enemy general.

"Did you see anything else?" he asked Evans.

"Yes, sir. I saw half a dozen flat-bottomed boats, each able to carry twenty men, hidden in inlets and along the shore, covered with brush and leaves. Who knows how many more there might be."

"It would perfectly ordinary for boats to be there," someone said. "They might plan to follow their main attack with an attack at Queenston."

"Or it might be a diversion, to draw off our troops from our flanks."

"I think they *wanted* Evans to see the boats, to fool him."

Evans kept his gaze on Brock, who continued to gaze at the wall. "Sir," Evans said quietly. "I am certain the Americans are about to attack, probably within a few hours. We must prepare."

The room was silent. Everyone watched Brock. He was like a pillar, standing there motionless, his one hand clenched against his chest, his eyes unfocused, staring through the wall, the night, the rain, toward the distant enemy. No one moved. We were all frozen in Brock's trance.

Then he was striding toward the door so quickly, almost violently, that several officers jumped.

"Evans, follow me."

They disappeared into a small room across the hall. The other officers looked at each other, shrugged their shoulders.

Someone called for port. The regular servant had disappeared, so I took over. It gave me an excuse to stay.

It was almost an hour later when Brock came back into the room. I had seen that grey, granite look only once before—in York, when he decided to move on Detroit.

"I am convinced the Americans are planning an attack, possibly tomorrow. Whether the main attack will come at Queenston or somewhere else we cannot know. We must be ready."

He delivered his orders in a stream, one to each officer. The local militia were to come to the fort tonight. The outlying militia were to rush to their posts as quickly as possible. All troops along the front were to be ready for an attack as early as dawn. The Indians were to be alerted, and told they might be needed at any moment. It went on, a river of commands.

"Evans." Brock turned back to the major. "What did you do with the Queenston mutineers?"

"I sent them back to their posts, sir." Evans shrugged. "It seemed a poor time to be arresting our own men."

Brock scowled, then the scowl disappeared and he laughed, he actually laughed. "If your prediction is correct, Evans, this could be the most fortunate mutiny in history. We shall have to decorate them.

"Gentlemen, we have a full night ahead."

All that night I delivered messages, orders, letters. I returned to Brock's quarters at three to find him slumped over his desk, asleep. I left him there, went to the stables, made sure Alfred was fed and his saddle nearby. I made sure another horse was ready too, one used by messengers riding between forts. Then I threw myself onto my bed. I dreamed of guns, and men dying, and horses screaming, and the endless roar of cannon. Over and over again I heard the cannon.

I half-awoke. There was a storm outside. Thunder grumbled in the far distance.

I jumped from my bed. The thunder was regular, repeated.

It was no dream. It *was* the sound of cannon.

The Americans had attacked.

18

I ran out of the barracks at the same moment Brock appeared from the officers' quarters. He sprinted across the parade ground toward the stables. I was there before him.

"Where's the saddle?"

"Here, sir."

He didn't wait for me to help, but threw the saddle over Alfred's back and cinched it tight. I was saddling the horse beside.

"Tell the other officers I am on my way to Queenston."

I looked up at him. "Sir, let me go with you. My horse is ready."

"I don't need you at Queenston." He wheeled Alfred toward the stable door.

"You do sir. You need a messenger. I'm the only one ready."

He paused for a second, then waved me onto my horse. "Follow me."

We rode through the gates of Fort George together, then turned south toward the artillery that roared five miles away.

It was still dark, and a cold sleet cut at our clothes. Brock's cloak was quickly spattered with mud; I was covered in it. But he ignored the sleet and the mud and pushed Alfred on.

I watched him, bent over his horse, staring out at the night. It was up to him now. He knew it—we all knew it. Our lives, our future, were up to him. I suddenly realized how lonely he must be, riding in the dark toward battle. I felt glad I was there with him.

A rider came charging down the road toward us. Brock raised his hand and the rider reined in his horse, though he was going so fast he almost got past us before he could stop. He was a young militia officer.

"Sir—" He was breathless. "The Americans have landed in force at Queenston."

"How many? Are they being opposed?" Brock leaned forward in his saddle.

"Yes sir," the officer said excitedly. "Our cannon on the heights are doing great damage. Their boats are sinking, or being forced downstream. Only a few hundred troops have made it to our side, and we have them pinned."

"Good," Brock replied. "Get to Fort George. Tell General Sheaffe to stand ready. This may be only a diversion."

"Yes sir." The officer saluted and we rode off in our different directions.

We were almost at Queenston when we came upon a company of militia marching toward the village. They were the York militia, the same men who had volunteered to follow Brock to Detroit. Now they were with him here. The general took off his hat and waved them toward the village.

They gave him a cheer in reply.

The eastern sky was streaked red with approaching dawn when we reached the village. Queenston was a collection of about a dozen houses surrounded by orchards and old stone fences. The village was already crowded with more than a hundred soldiers from the 49th regiment. They were Brock's favourite. He'd been with them for years, and had brought them down from Kingston for the battle. They shouted and cheered as he rode past them.

Brock pushed Alfred up the slope from the village to the heights that overlooked the river. He ignored the steady stream of cannon fire that poured across from the American side onto the slope and into the village.

Even before we reached the crest the sound of the battle had become deafening. When we got to the top we saw why. The American artillery was positioned directly across from us on the American heights. Volley after volley of grapeshot poured across the sky. The American village of Lewiston was choked with regiments of American troops. Below us a handful of our militia were pouring a deadly fire on several hundred Yankees who huddled defenceless at the bottom of the cliff. Our own cannon was sending shot at the wide, flat boats that every now and then launched from the American shore and tried to cross the river.

The gorge below us was filled with smoke and fog and dying men. The rising sun showed bodies floating face-down in the swirling waters of the Niagara. Downstream, American soldiers struggled onto shore, some in the remains of their shattered boats, some swimming for their lives. They were quickly taken prisoner.

It was an inferno in the gorge. To the Americans trapped under our fire, it must have been like Hell itself.

Brock dismounted and led Alfred down a steep slope to our cannon. From our militia below an officer came scrambling up the slope to meet him.

"General Brock, Captain Dennis at your service, sir." He saluted, but couldn't keep a grin off his face. "I think we have them, sir."

Brock shook his head, puzzled. "What's the matter with them? They have thousands of men over there. But they just sit. Why don't they cross?"

"Lack of boats, I think." Dennis had to shout to make himself heard over the roar of the cannon. "And they may not want to cross, after seeing what happened to the first wave."

Brock gazed down on the Americans huddled at the base of the cliff. Most of them were wounded, crouched among their own dead, using them for shelter. I had never seen dead and wounded soldiers before. The sight of it made my head go light. I stepped back, afraid I might be sick.

Brock was unmoved. He was used to battlefields. "Dennis," he said, pointing. "Is there any way those men can scale these cliffs and come at us from behind?"

Dennis shook his head. "No sir. There's only one path from the landing to the village, and we have it covered. There's no path straight up the cliff."

"Good." Brock waved to a company of infantry that had appeared at the crest of the heights above the cannon. An officer hurried forward.

"Send word to Fort George and to Chippawa in the south." Brock's voice was calm, almost quiet. "Tell them to send reinforcements." He looked out at the thousands of Americans on the far shore. "Evans was right. This is no diversion. This is the main attack." He turned back to the officer. "Take your men down the cliff to where the militia are stationed and support their fire on the troops landing at the dock."

"Yes sir." The officer saluted and hurried off. Brock turned his attention to the cannon beside us. Some of the shells were falling short. He started giving orders on how to improve the range.

I never saw them, Brock never saw them. They came from nowhere—not nowhere, they came along a path that wound up the cliff—the path that everyone had said didn't exist, except the Americans knew it did. We heard a shout, and then a ragged cheer behind us. Brock wheeled around. Maybe sixty Americans were rushing toward us from the top of the crest above. In the pale morning light their bayonets glowed dull and deadly.

"Spike the cannon!" Brock shouted. If the Americans got the use of our artillery, they could pour shot down on our troops directly below. A young gunner shoved a metal spike into the cannon's powder hole. Now the cannon was useless.

"Follow me!" Brock grabbed Alfred's reins and led the gun crew away from the cannon. In a moment we were scrambling down the hill toward the village. A roar went up from the other side of the river. The Americans had seen their own troops on the heights.

The battle had turned.

We fell back to the village, but the American cannon from across the river rained shot down on the houses more fiercely than ever. The balls crashed through the shingled roofs, set fires burning, smashed stone. The few civilians who hadn't fled cowered in their root cellars. Dust and smoke surrounded everything. Dennis, the militia captain, was wounded; so were many of his men. Brock pulled the troops—maybe two hundred of us now—back to the far edge of the village.

We huddled there, under the American cannon fire, watching as more and more Yankee soldiers appeared at the crest of the heights to reinforce the men already there. A moment ago the battle was ours—the Americans pinned down, trapped, most of them afraid even to cross the river. Now they were in command. They owned the heights and had us pinned in the village. Brock was losing the battle.

I crouched behind a stone fence, terrified. I'd never been under fire before. Every cannon shot stabbed at my nerves. I wanted to flatten myself against the stone until I became part of it. I wanted to be away from here, anywhere but in the middle of this deadly fire. I had followed Brock to Queenston because it was my duty, but mostly because I wanted to watch Brock win. But this was not Detroit—the Yankees had us.

He was only a few feet from me, behaving the same as he ever did. He ignored the grapeshot that whistled about him. His face was calm, his voice steady. Except I noticed he was clenching and unclenching his left fist, over and over, which I'd never seen him do before.

Dennis crawled up beside Brock. He was bleeding in the leg and shoulder, his face ashen.

"Sir," he gasped, "are reinforcements coming?"

Brock nodded. "They're coming, but they'll be too late. The Americans grow stronger each minute. We must counter-attack."

Dennis's jaw dropped. "Sir, we have barely two hundred men. We've lost our cannon. They have the high ground. An attack will fail."

Brock shook his head. "Not if pressed forward with determination." He looked toward the heights. "If the Americans control the heights, they control the village. They will be able to move their entire army across. They will winter here, growing stronger each week. By the time spring comes it will be impossible to defeat them.

"If we do not win the heights back now, we will have lost the war."

Dennis nodded. He seemed unconvinced, but Brock was the general. And Dennis had already been wrong about the path up the cliff.

Brock walked swiftly over to a nearby house. I had tethered Alfred there, behind the far wall for safety. Suddenly he appeared in front of us, mounted on Alfred, the cannon whistling past.

"Follow me, boys!" he shouted. "Follow me! We shall defeat them yet!"

He shook Alfred's reins and the two of them moved gravely forward. The men looked at each other and some groaned, but they rose from behind their shelters and fell into formation behind him.

I didn't want to leave the safety of the fence. I didn't

want to stand before their cannon and muskets and die. But Brock was at the front. How could I cower here while he marched off toward the enemy? What would he think of me?

I looked along the fence. A militia man sprawled dead on the ground, a mass of red flesh where his face had been. My stomach heaved, and I choked and swallowed hard. He had a musket, and I needed a musket. I crawled along the fence toward him, grabbed the musket, pulled the canvas satchel of balls and powder from around his neck, wiped off the blood, and ran toward the troops ahead.

At the base of the slope rising up to the crest of the heights was a stone fence. Brock had already dismounted and was crouching behind it. The men filed in along either side. In the bush above the Yankee infantry kept a steady fire over our heads.

Brock looked at the soldiers and militia huddled together. "Take a breath, boys," he called out. "You'll need it in a moment."

A ragged cheer ran down the line.

I crouched a few feet away from Brock, my musket clenched in my shaking hands. Suddenly Brock was beside me, prying the musket away. "Batmen don't fight," he said quietly. "Who would press my uniform if you were shot? Stay with Alfred."

"Please, sir." I swallowed. "I need to be here."

He paused for a moment, looked at me, then handed back the musket, and rested his hand lightly on my shoulder. "Good luck, son."

I tried to grin. "Good luck, General."

He tried to grin back. "Good luck to us both."

Then he stood, pulled his sword from his sheath, and pointed it toward the hill.

"Forward!"

In an instant he was over the fence, striding up the slope. We scrambled over the fence behind him, trying to catch up.

There was no time to form a proper line. We fanned out behind Brock, marching up the steep slope of the hill toward the crest. The ground was slick with wet leaves. It was hard to keep our footing. Ahead of us, at the top of the hill, the Americans clustered around the captured cannon. Others crouched in nearby bushes. Both kept up a steady fire. A man groaned and fell beside me. Another, directly ahead, clutched his side and fell to the ground. I stepped over him, tried not to think, tried to push back the fear.

But we were getting closer. Our line held behind Brock. I saw blood trickling from his hand—he'd been nicked there by a musket ball. But he ignored the wound and pushed forward, his sabre drawn, calling to the men to follow.

The Americans fell back to the edge of the cliff. They hadn't expected a frontal attack, were frightened by the determined troops who slipped and stumbled up the hill toward them, ignoring their fire. I saw someone pull out a white handkerchief and begin to wave it. An officer struck it down with a curse, pulled out his sword and pointed it toward us. The Americans charged.

We didn't expect it. Their commander had the same blood in his veins as Brock did. He had his back to a cliff, nowhere to go, so he charged.

They fired as they marched down the hill toward us.

Men fell. The troops behind Brock turned their backs on the Yankees, began to retreat down the hill. Brock swivelled around, saw his men falling back, and cried out.

"Not the 49th! The 49th never turns its back!"

The men hesitated, unsure. The Americans were advancing. Men were dying everywhere. But Brock was there, calling them to follow. Brock, who the men had never disobeyed, who had given them victory, who they loved in a way, the way soldiers love a general they trust. The men looked at each other. Should they die for him?

For an instant the sun came out. Gold glinted off the wet leaves and grass. I looked up the hill. Brock was maybe three steps away, his sword drawn, calling out to the wavering British line.

"Forward, men!" he shouted to us. "Forward!"

The sun gleamed off his epaulettes, glowed off the silver blade of his sword. For a moment everything seemed suspended, the battle hanging in the air like the smoke from our muskets.

I saw the Yankee soldier kneeling, saw him sight down his barrel, saw the flash and puff of smoke.

Brock stopped in mid-stride. His sword fell from his hand. I watched it fall—it seemed forever—onto the wet grass below. He sank to his knees, then pitched forward, his face buried in the glistening leaves.

"*NO!*" I stumbled forward, fell, pushed myself on, reached him, got my hands on his shoulders, rolled him over. His face was lifeless. A red stain spread across his scarlet tunic, darkening it to blood red.

Brock was dead.

19

We carried his body down the hill, the musket balls whistling over our heads. The weight of him strained at my shoulders, and my sweat mixed with my tears. *He's dead. He's dead.*

Once we were back behind the fence several officers gathered around him. One placed a mirror above his mouth. If it steamed that would be a sign Brock was breathing. But another officer pushed the mirror away. There was no hope.

One of the militia commanders began ordering us to form up again. His name was Macdonell, and with Brock dead he was now senior officer.

"We'll attack again," he shouted, walking up and down the line. "We'll avenge the general!"

I didn't care if we attacked. If we attacked again, we'd probably die. I didn't care if we all died.

A hand gently touched my arm. "Not you, lad. You stay with the general." A young officer looked down at me gravely. "That's your duty, now."

"Form your line!" Macdonell had taken his horse over the fence. He swung himself into the saddle and pulled out his sword. "Forward, men!" he cried. "Remember the General! Remember General Brock!"

But no more than fifty men leaped over the fence to join him. The rest stayed where they were, wounded, exhausted, defeated.

The small, ragged line advanced up the hill behind the colonel, stepping over the bodies of their own men. Before they got halfway the Americans opened fire. Macdonell's horse screamed and fell. Then Macdonell collapsed. The line wavered, and broke. Men began to run back toward the fence.

The British officers had no more stomach for assaults. We were pulled back to the rear of the village. Three of us carried Brock into a stone house, then left him to find Alfred. He would be worried about Alfred. The horse was standing outside the house, motionless, staring silently at the door. I tethered him behind the house, out of danger. It was the last thing I was able to do on my own. I slid down the wall beside the horse and closed my eyes. I was empty.

Brock is dead. No. Yes. He fell—you saw him. You carried him. No, I didn't. It was a mistake. You saw him fall. He's dead. . . .

I sat in the mud, my back against the wall. Men around me wept and cursed the Yankees and swore revenge, but I didn't hear them. *Everyone's dead. We're all going to be dead. I want to be dead. . . .*

The battle was lost. The Americans were sending troops across the river, reinforcing their position on the heights. Most of our cannon had been knocked out of action. We were pinned in the village, too few to attack. Any time now, the Yankees would pour down into the village, and some of us would surrender and the rest of us would die.

"Form up! We're moving out." Officers were among us, rousing the men. Were we going to attack again? Was I to die on the hill like Brock?

But we weren't going to attack. We were leaving the village, going beyond the range of the cannon. Before long we were in the bush behind the town, marching west up a steep hill. It seemed strange—Fort George was to the north. Why weren't we going back to Fort George? I didn't care. *March me anywhere. Let me fight. Brock is dead. . . .*

But the sight when we came out of the bush woke me up. Hundreds of British troops, scarlet uniforms row on row, stood in a ploughed field. Flags snapped in the breeze, officers on horses galloped about shouting orders. The reinforcements from Chippawa and Fort George had arrived, but whoever was replacing Brock had decided to keep away from the village. He was preparing his attack in safety, waiting until everything was in place. Brock would never have been so cautious.

Beside them were rows of militia, the men wearing whatever they threw on when word came of the attack. Their faces were grim, hard. They'd heard of Brock's death. He was their general too, and they wanted blood.

We fell into the line, near one end. Everyone seemed to think I was another private, part of the 49th regiment. I let them think it.

Behind us, on a great black horse, sat a British general. Sheaffe—I had seen him at Fort George. People said he was conservative, by the book, the opposite of Brock.

For two hours we waited. Sheaffe was massing every

troop he could find, waiting until the last reinforcements arrived before attacking, forming his lines in perfect order. By the book.

"Let's get on with it," someone muttered. Sheaffe continued to wait.

But there was no need to hurry. From the bush surrounding the Yankees came howls and screams and musket shot. The Mohawk. I imagined the Yankee soldiers, listening to the war cries in the bush. What were those sounds doing to them? What were they thinking? I was sure that the longer we waited, the more frightened the Yankees would be.

"Fix bayonets!"

At last Sheaffe was ready to attack. There were almost a thousand of us—but who could know how many Americans had poured across the river in the hours since Brock's death? Well, we'd find out soon.

"Forward!"

We marched across the field, the Mohawk running from the bush to join our flank. On the far side we could see the Yankees. I'd expected more of them. They'd had hours to reinforce. But there were no more than a couple hundred, dug in behind piles of earth. They had wasted their time.

We marched forward steadily, our boots sinking into the wet earth of the field, the drums beating out the pace.

I wasn't sweating any more. I clenched my musket in cold determination. They killed Brock. I wanted to reach them. I wanted to kill. For the first time in my life, I wanted to kill.

Brock is dead.

The Americans opened fire, but there were too few of them, and we were still too far away.

Suddenly the Indians gave a great battle cry and rushed forward. In their hands they clenched muskets, in their belts, tomahawks—eager for the scalps of the Long Knives.

It was too much for the Yankees. Men began running away toward the cliff. I saw an officer waving his sword, shouting at the men to stand their ground, but he was pushed back by a wave of deserters.

A group of them held their ground, maybe a few dozen at the most. Our line approached. I could see their faces—frightened of death, frightened of disgrace.

"Attack with bayonets!"

I plunged forward, my musket thrust out in front of me. In a moment, we were at the earthworks. I leaped over them. There was a flash of blue, of steel. Without thinking, I thrust my musket at it. The bayonet sank into something soft, like sand.

I froze. He was no older than I was. His eyes stared at me, his mouth open. Then he sank to the earth, my bayonet still in his chest, the blood soaking his shirt. *My God!* I yanked at the bayonet, pulled it out of him. He fell backward, sprawled on the ground, his eyes still wide open, dead.

Suddenly I was vomiting, unable to stop. I bent over, retched, retched again. Then I staggered away. No matter what happened, I couldn't stand to look at him again.

The Americans who survived our charge were falling back. I rejoined the line, already at the top of the cliff. Below was chaos. The Indians were pouring down the hill, burying their hatchets into the skulls of every Yankee they reached. Some Americans had thrown themselves from the cliffs in panic—you could see their twisted bodies on the banks below. Others were trying to swim across the churning river. I saw one head disappear, then another. Dozens of men huddled on the bank by the river, many of them without muskets, waiting in terror for the Indians.

An American officer marched up the hill, escorted by two militiamen. They brought him to Sheaffe. A minute later the bugle sounded cease-fire. But the Mohawks ignored the bugle. They had come to kill. Sheaffe himself had to beg their chief to stop before they reluctantly put their tomahawks back in their belts.

I looked across the river. Thousands of Americans lined the shore, row on row of blue, silently watching their comrades surrender. Why hadn't they crossed?

An Indian jumped on a rock and raised his arms. Head back, bare skin glistening in the rain, he screamed bloody defiance to the men across the river. A few swore back. Most turned away.

The American army of the Niagara—eight thousand strong—had refused to go into battle. They were frightened, poorly led. And terrified of being scalped.

And then I knew. Brock didn't need to die. If he'd waited until the Indians arrived, he would have had his victory and still be alive. The charge up the hill had been a mistake.

I covered my face with my hands. I had seen too much today. I had killed a man. I had seen men slaughtered.

Brock you died—for nothing.

They took his body back to Fort George, and five thousand soldiers, militia, and Indians, muskets upside-down in tribute, stood in line as the coffin passed by.

There had been no celebrating after the victory. Brock's death had stolen our victory from us. After the battle most of the soldiers just wandered about, talking among themselves, asking, Did you see it? Were you there? What happened?

I talked to no one and no one talked to me. Most of the time I spent near Alfred, endlessly brushing and grooming him. He was all of Brock I had left.

After the funeral I wandered away from the soldiers and mourners and began to walk. I walked along the bank of the river, stared out at the green waters of the Niagara, and thought about Brock.

He had often been cold to me, but never cruel. Mostly he had asked only that I serve him, and I had served him as well as I could.

I thought about the day I left the farm—it seemed like

years ago now. I was so different. I had killed a man, watched him die. I had seen a man I loved killed.

I stopped, and closed my eyes.

I had loved Brock. He had taught me, looked after me when I was supposed to be looking after him, shown me what strength was, shown me how the strongest among us are weak.

When I first met him he asked me if I were a good man. I'd said—what had I said? I'd said I hoped I was good enough.

He liked that answer. He would have liked it. That's what he wanted for himself—to be good enough to win, to be good enough to win respect.

Maitland told me that soldiers eat bad food and sleep on the ground and march and fight and die.

Brock was a soldier. It was part of who he was to die like that. That was how he was supposed to die.

I turned away from the river, and walked back to the fort.

The order to see Captain Stanton came early the next morning. I hurried over to the officers' quarters. I hadn't seen him since Detroit. I didn't want to see him now.

"Sit down, private." It was a surprising order. Privates stood in front of officers. I had never heard a captain ask a private to sit.

Stanton was sorting through a great pile of papers. This was a time officers hated. The battle was over, winter was coming on, there were supplies to order, men to clothe and

house through the winter months, nothing interesting—
like war—to do.

Stanton shuffled through his papers and pulled out a
letter. He looked at it thoughtfully for a moment, then put
it down.

"Do you know how to read, private?"

I nodded. "Yes sir."

"You'll remember I was the officer who recommended
you as General Brock's batman. It was a risk, but an
interesting risk."

I sat stiffly in the chair, watching him. I should be
standing. Sitting was wrong. Why had he asked me to sit?

"Were you happy, serving General Brock?" Stanton
asked.

"Sir? I . . . yes, sir. Very happy." Happy was the wrong
word, but I didn't know the right one, and wouldn't have
said it out loud if I did.

"General Brock was . . . impressed with your work."
Stanton glanced down at the letter on his desk. "He gave me
this letter some days before . . . before the battle at
Queenston Heights, and asked me to open it in the event
he . . . " Stanton coughed. " . . . in the event he was killed."

Stanton rubbed his eyes. It was only the day after the
funeral.

"I was . . . surprised by this request, I must tell you. I did
not know the general well, at least no better than any of the
other officers, some of whom are quite senior to me. But I
see now why I was entrusted with it."

He handed the letter to me across the desk. "Here, read
it."

I recognized the handwriting at once—Brock's script was broad and clear. The letter was dated September 30th, two weeks ago. It was strange, seeing words written by him. It was strange reading in front of an officer. But I'd been told to read.

The words were hard—I didn't even know what some of them meant. But the meaning was clear.

Captain Stanton,

Some months ago I asked you to procure for me from the ranks a private to serve as my batman. As you will recall, I expressed misgivings concerning your nomination of the colonial volunteer Jeremy Fields. The boy appeared too young and inexperienced even for this admittedly less than onerous task.

However, I have been impressed by the service of Private Fields and wish to express my gratitude for your perspicacious choice. He has served me well and is a valuable, if at times impertinent, aide.

I sense the boy is capable of greater achievement than he has been given opportunity to display heretofore. I am taking the liberty, therefore, of asking you this favour.

Since, if you are reading this, misfortune shall have fallen upon me and I am no longer able to execute my own affairs, I would deem it a great service if you would attend to the proper education of Fields. I have instructed my solicitors in London, in the event of my death, to set aside a sum of five hundred pounds, in trust, to be used to defray the costs of bringing Fields to England and supporting him while he pursues his studies. I believe he has had little formal schooling, and it may be some years before he is able to pursue whatever vocation awaits him.

If you would see to it that my wishes have been carried out, and expedite Fields's discharge from His Majesty's service, and attend to those necessary details such as his transportation to England and accommodation once there (I fear these tasks would be daunting for one of such purely colonial experience), I will owe you a great debt, which, obviously, I shall be unable to repay.

Please accept my deepest apologies for placing this burden upon your shoulders, and accept also my sincerest gratitude for your services. I remain,

Your humble and obedient servant,

Isaac Brock

"Do you understand the letter?" Stanton asked.

I nodded. I didn't trust myself to speak.

Stanton rose from his chair. "Very well, then. I will see to the details. You will need tutoring in England before you will be ready for any other education. I will also arrange for your accommodation there. It will take a week, I should think, to arrange your discharge. Until then, consider yourself on leave. When would you like to depart for England?"

I shook my head. "Whenever . . . whenever you want."

"It should be soon. The Atlantic is not an ocean best crossed in winter. There is a ship sailing from Quebec City in three weeks. Can you be there?"

"Yes."

"Then we'll try for that date. Have you any questions?"

I had only one. "Sir, can I keep the letter?"

Stanton paused. "I had rather hoped to keep it myself. He . . . we were all devoted to him you know." He cleared his throat. "But the letter is about you, and it really belongs to you. Yes, take the letter."

I stood up and snapped to attention. "Will that be all, sir?"

"Yes. Return here in one week. That will be all, Fields."

"Sir." I pivoted sharply about-face. I was exaggerating everything I did, hoping it would keep me in control.

"Fields . . . " Stanton's voice came from behind.

I swung around. "Sir?"

He stood behind his desk, head bent over, examining some paper. "I . . . I'm rather proud that I chose you to be the general's batman."

He didn't look up. I swallowed, tried to say something, but there was nothing to say. We knew what we were thinking. I closed the door softly behind me.

The next morning I left Fort George and set out for the farm. In the past five months I had gone through war and seen death and served a great man. Now I was going to England. It was time to say a proper goodbye to my home.

The walk was colder than in May, and longer, but I didn't mind. I was tougher than I was then and used to marching mile upon mile. A grey wind whipped at the flaps of my cloak, but I ignored it.

The fields were bare, as they had been bare then. But they were lifeless now. The harvest was in, and only the stubble of the crops littered the brown earth. I saw no one. The farmers were in the barns or in their homes. They had no call to be out in the fields.

I stayed the first night at the village where Brock had given his speech, and the second night at York. The next morning, before the sun had fully lightened the flat clouds covering the sky, I set out for the farm. I walked slowly. Five months ago I travelled down this road harbouring a rage for a man who had stolen my mother's farm for twenty pounds. I had wanted to kill him. Now I *had* killed, killed a man I didn't know, who probably didn't deserve to die.

I found it hard to remember the rage.

It was past noon when I walked up the path to the house. As soon as I saw it I knew no one lived there now. The doors to the barn were open, creaking in the wind. The barn was empty. I walked across the muddy yard to the house. A window was broken, the door ajar. I stepped inside. The furniture was gone. It was as though no one had ever lived here, as though the place had been abandoned the day it was built.

There was an empty box—we'd kept wood in it—against one wall. I pulled it into the middle of the room and sat down.

I tried to imagine my mother here, moving quietly about, a bowl in her hand, her apron tied about her. I tried to imagine this room filled with light from the fire, the smell of baking scenting the air, the snow beating uselessly against the window, everything inside warm and safe.

I had never said goodbye to her. She never knew what became of her son. Had she known she was dying? Did she rage against it, as I had raged against Uncle Will? Maybe not. She had made a home and produced a child, and raised him, and given everything she had to give to those who needed her.

I'm all right, mama.

"Who's there?"

I jumped. A figure framed the doorway. It was dark in the room, but there was enough light to make out the musket pointing at me.

"Who are you?" the figure asked again. "What are you doing here?"

I knew the voice now. "This is my home, Uncle Will."

"Jeremy?" He lowered the musket and stepped into the room. "Jeremy, it *is* you. My God, you gave me a fright. Seth came running to the house, said he'd seen some soldier going in here. You never know, in these times . . . ."

He was talking too fast, and the nervousness in his voice made it quaver a bit.

"So." He leaned the musket against the wall, but kept near it. "You're a soldier."

"Yes."

"Have you fought in the war?"

"Yes. I was batman to General Brock."

His eyes widened. "*You?* That takes some believing, boy."

"It doesn't matter if you believe it or not."

Was this the man I had wanted to kill? I hadn't noticed before the fat under the chin, the belly that fell over the belt. Had I really hated this man?

"What are you . . . why did you come back?" he asked.

He was frightened. Had I come for his land? Had I told some British officer about him? Was the law coming? Had I really known Brock? How much trouble was he in?

"I came back to see the place. I'm leaving for England. I wanted to say goodbye to the house."

Did he know he sighed so loudly I could hear it?

"Oh. Off to England. Is your regiment returning there?"

"No. I'm going to school."

I didn't want to talk any more. I had done what I came to do. I wanted to get out of this ghost of a house, off this land that had no life. I started toward the door. Uncle Will stepped backwards, out into the yard.

"Here." He'd forgotten his musket. I handed it to him. Fear darted across his eyes when he saw me holding the gun. He grabbed it away from me, then smiled an apology.

"Well, it was good to see you again, Jeremy. You must come back here, when you return from England."

He didn't want me back. He didn't want to see my face again. He wanted the ship to sink in the middle of the ocean with all hands.

"Goodbye, uncle." I started down the path, then stopped. "Uncle Will."

He stood there, holding the musket against his chest.

"Yes, Jeremy?"

"I want the family Bible."

He opened his mouth, then closed it. He was going to tell me it was his, that he was head of the family now, that I had no right to it. But then he thought of what might happen if he refused. What was a Bible, if it would get rid of me? There were plenty of Bibles, and he had the money to buy them.

"If you want it, son, you're welcome to it."

"Have Seth bring it to me. I'll be on the road."

I turned my back on him, on the farm, on the dead past, and walked away.

Epilogue

I am sitting at a desk in a tent on the banks of a river called the Rideau. We are building a canal—a great canal from Kingston to the Ottawa River. The generals say we need it to move troops between Upper and Lower Canada, in case the Americans invade again.

Almost twenty years it's been, and still we worry about invasion. The war, of course, is over, but people fear another could come. The Americans go to war as easily as lighting a pipe—with the Spanish, with the Indians, with us.

Myself, I'm not sure we need the canal. The Americans have left us alone since the War of 1812. I think they've given up on owning all the continent.

But it doesn't really matter. For me the pleasure is in the building—I let the politicians decide what needs to be built.

I didn't see the last two years of the war. There was a lot of fighting. They attacked York and burned it. We attacked and burned Washington. We lost Detroit. They took Niagara, then lost it.

The only news from the war that really mattered to me was hearing of Tecumseh's death. After the Yankees recaptured Detroit they moved up the Thames Valley. The British and Indians met them at a place called Moraviantown. When the British saw they were going to lose they surrendered. But Tecumseh kept the Indians fighting, until finally he was killed, and his warriors disappeared into the bush. Their hopes for their land disappeared with them.

It was 1814 before both sides got tired of the killing and decided to quit. The reasons for the war were long forgotten. Napoleon had been defeated, and the ports of Europe were open. Neither side had won any land they could hold on to. The politicians decided to return both countries to their old borders.

The war, I think, never really meant much to the Yankees. They dreamed of grabbing half a continent without having to fire a shot. When they realized it would be harder than that they gave up, and went back to conquering the west.

The farmers of Upper Canada returned to their fields, more worried about the crops than the country. But they were never quite the same again. They had proved they were different from the Americans. Maybe they shared the same language, the same religion, even the same ancestors. But they weren't Americans, and didn't want to be Americans, and were willing to fight to preserve the difference.

They won their fight. They were probably the only winners in the entire war.

But the war, when it ended, was already far from me. I was living in London, in a house run by a woman who never smiled and never put any salt in the potatoes, getting an education.

It was lonely in London, at first. I was homesick, which was strange because I had no home. London was enormous. All those people crammed together, and I didn't know one of them and not one of them wanted to know me.

But I knew I was there for a reason. Brock had given me a chance—a chance to choose my life instead of having it chosen for me. I wasn't going to waste that chance. I got on. I discovered I was good with numbers—better than good. I could see into them where others just stared and didn't understand. Eventually I entered a school for army engineers. I still had this dream of seeing all those capitals on the map in the back of my Bible.

I've seen some of them. I've built roads across a baked Indian plain, rounded the cape that marks the end of Africa, cut my way through the Jamaican bush, crossed the desert sands of Australia.

I have fallen in love, and then out of it, and then moved on before I could fall into it again.

And now I'm back in Upper Canada, helping to build this canal. And I'm thinking of Brock.

He's never really left my mind. In the army, whenever I meet a new officer, I measure him against Brock. I've never met a man who matched him.

Brock is worshipped now. They call him the Saviour of Upper Canada. There's a great monument built in his memory at Queenston Heights. People talk of him as though he were some kind of saint.

I can never think of him that way. When I think of Brock I think of a general in a kitchen, showing a fifteen-year-old boy how to make a roast beef sandwich. I think of him leaping out of a boat into dark waters to push it free of a rock. I think of him sitting in his cabin on the *Chippawa*, amazed at the impudent batman who dares question him, and then struggling to answer the question.

He was a decent man, who knew what he had to do, and tried to do it. And if others say the same of me, that will be good enough.

Time to stop. It's after midnight, and we start work at dawn.

I have work to do.

ACKNOWLEDGEMENTS

Although some artistic licence has been necessary—Brock's servant, Thomas Porter, did not die before Brock—I've tried to make the events in this book as historically accurate as possible. In this effort I was greatly helped by the contributions of Professors Stanley Wise of Carleton University, Wesley Turner of Brock University, and Paul Cornell of the University of Waterloo (retired). Their meticulous reviews of the manuscript, and the many comments and suggestions they offered, improved *1812* enormously. Any errors or oversights that remain are my own.

I am also very grateful to Mary Lloyd, of the Richmond Hill Public Library, for her great assistance, especially with the opening chapters of the book; to Michael Butler, of George Harvey CI in Toronto, for his helpful advice on making the work suitable for school use; and to the young reviewers, whose comments on *1812* were both valuable and encouraging.

And I owe a special debt to Karen Alliston, my editor, for her devotion and insight. Without her, Brock and Jeremy would not have been who they are.

Finally, I would like to offer thanks to Patrick Gallagher, editorial director at Maxwell Macmillan, for asking me if I would like to write a novel, to president Ray Lee, for his faith in the project, and to all my friends at that excellent house.

This book is about a time in this nation's past when our very existence was threatened. We are threatened again, but today we are our own enemy. If Canada is to endure, if the sacrifice of those who fought and died nearly two hundred years ago is to have any final meaning, then it is for us to fight—peacefully and passionately and with all our strength—to preserve our country.

We owe them no less.

Ottawa
June 2, 1991